Pawn

The Broken Bows, Volume 3

Kerri Ann

Published by Kerri Ann, 2018.

PAWN

First edition. August 23, 2018.

Copyright © 2018 Kerri Ann.

ISBN: 979-8224849116

Written by Kerri Ann.

Also by Kerri Ann

The Broken Bows
Rook

King

Pawn

Watch for more at https://www.authorkerriann.com.

Chapter One

B<u>usta</u>

"Why isn't someone doing something?" I shout.

Seething mad at the imbecilic prospects and fearful members that surround me, I race like the chariots of hell are on my heels. Arriving to a fucking catastrophe, I move swiftly to the front doors, just as Miss strolls out with Smart. Miss's shirt is freshly stained with blood, and a bandage is visible just below his right shoulder.

"You good, brother?" I ask Miss.

"Yeah. Fuckin' flesh wound. I've had worse." He winces slightly as he rolls his shoulder around.

Hearing the rundown of what happened, and knowing that Miss survived a run-in with Strike, Smart comments tentatively, "Sorry, Busta. We didn't know what to do. We weren't allowed to ride along to the hospital because the fucking cops blocked the street and kept us for questioning."

"'Course they did." I look around. "Where's Scarlet? Did she go with the ambo?" I ask, knowing she should be by True and Strike's sides. They've been lovers, family, and friends since they were teens.

Taking a step back, Smart shakes his head. "She went with True to the parish, but since then, she's disappeared."

Flight gives me the rundown. It seems that after I'd left, True and Strike had a heated conversation. Miss pissed off Strike, causing him to shoot a bolt through his shoulder. Strike then took off down the street with his famous bow in tow.

It seems that True played his brother, and as always, Scarlet was at the center of it all.

Now both brothers are at the hospital in critical condition, fighting for their lives, which leaves me as acting Pres. Something I'm sure was orchestrated by King in some twisted way.

Everything is going wrong. "This is a major fucking mess!"

Hearing Miss mutter his agreement, I rake my hand through my thick beard. I'm beyond frustrated. I'm set to commit murder.

"Going after the VP's family was just stupid. True knew better," Miss states. Regret is useless, especially seeing that it's so close to the truth.

Magnus King had his hand in this; I'm sure of it.

Palming the grip of my gun, it calls for me to fire at anything that moves. I'm reaching my limit of giving any fucks today.

"Busta, another thing. There was a note at the front gates." Smart reaches into his cut and pulls it out. Handing it over to me, I flip it over and read.

King said to say 'Hi'.

Death

He's working with King?

I swear, if Death had something to do with this power change, nothing will stop me from raining hell down on him. I'll give him the benefit of the doubt right now, because in my gut I suspect King is behind it all. Death and I had a truce, an understanding—and if he's balled up in this bag of shit, no one in the Army will be left standing.

"Mount up," I say, straddling my bike.

Hitting the throttle, I don't turn to see if others are behind me; I know they are.

Riding as fast as I can to the hospital, I think of everything as I attempt to un-puzzle this mess. This all happened over True fucking with the status quo.

Don't fuck with family.

Don't steal from your own yard.

Don't break bread with the man you offered peace to then stab him in the back.

True fucked this shit up.

And King? King is trying my patience.

Knowing I shouldn't have called him is hindsight. I can't do a thing about it now. I should've found my own way to help Oubliette and Jasmine. There are always two ways to fix things, and I fucked it further without even trying.

God dammit!

I *knew* there was something wrong with how fast King answered the call. He offered to help all to easily. I knew it smelled fuckin' wrong.

I should've gone with my gut.

He'll pay in blood if it's the last thing I do. They all will. The Hade's Army for the attack on True and Strike. The Heartless Bastards that jumped our supply, leaving Diesel in a coma, and the fucking DEA who put me in this position over ten years ago— in that order.

Though that cunt, Magnus King, will feel this the most.

He's going to pay.

Chapter Two

Busta

I hit the hospital parking lot with five brothers behind me. Two will be stationed with True and Strike, and two are for me. I didn't get much of a choice in it. They're here because I *supposedly* need protection now.

As the acting head of our club, I could've waved them off. I didn't, though. Thing is, after the meet with King, I have the feeling we shouldn't travel light anywhere. He's still planning something, that sick fuck.

Pulling in and parking, I see this is a moment of homemade chaos. Four bikes—two I instantly recognize as Army, and a transport van.

"True, remember?" Flight pipes up. "I hear Curse was at his brother-in-law's shop, protecting his family. He took a big hit trying to cover his niece and sister."

Fucking up family always leads to bigger problems. Families are off-limits, and this is why. You find it back on your own doorstep.

Leaving my bike, I start for the door. "Keep on your guard then, boys."

Arriving at the desk, the tiny woman behind it goes still. "I'm looking for two men that were brought in, Bracken and Kyden Madox. Could you give me their statuses?"

Clearing her throat, she asks, "Are you family?"

"The closest they've got." With DG dead, I'm it.

"So that's a no."

I'm losing my patience. I don't have time for bullshit today. "Sweetheart, tell me where they're at while I'm still calm. Last thing you want to be is the person who tells me no today."

"Is there a problem here?" Another woman pipes up. Tall, dark, and in control—obviously. She stands with her arms crossed over her chest.

"I need to know where the Madox brothers are." Leaning on the counter, staring her down, her stance remains defiant, so I continue. "I can tear this place down, or you can give me what I want, now."

Her stubbornness reminds me of my mother. Jet-black hair pulled tight to her scalp in a bun, wide hoop earrings, understated make-up, but overstated outfit, she knows she's in charge and expects me to bend. "You bikers don't scare me. You're not the first, and you're definitely not the first today to come at me."

Laying my piece on the desk, I grin. "I'll find them myself then, shall I?"

There are Army here. I'd normally leave my piece in the side bag, but with them in the same vicinity, I made sure we came locked and loaded.

Death and I had an understanding, but after this mess, that shit is out the window. I trust he cares for his club as much as I do mine.

Taking a step back, she changes her tone quick. "Second floor. ICU wing."

"Good choice, lady." Turning to the boys, I place my gun back in my waistband. "You heard the woman. Let's go."

Walking down the hall, we're given hard looks. People step to the side as we pass, and we stay alert. Two floors later, arriving at ICU, three Army are standing by a doorway. Death recognizes me immediately.

Giving me a look full of malice and contempt, he yells, "You!" Rising off the wall, he starts toward me. "You better turn right back the way you came, Busta. My patience is short after today."

I don't answer him, but continue on toward the ICU desk. I came for my club, and him pissing a line in the sand won't stop me. Turning to the frightened little woman behind the desk, I bark out, "Kyden and Bracken Madox. What are their conditions?"

Checking her paperwork, she looks up at me. "Both are in surgery, but it's not good."

Shit.

"I hope that piece of shit dies," Death comments rather loudly, trying my patience of diplomacy. He and his boys are a few doors down, and the space between us suits me just fine. But if he walks down while I'm dealing with this, I can't be sure we won't throw down.

In all honesty, I feel for Death. This has to be pulling him apart. I never thought of him as a bad guy, but I won't show fear or back down if he starts something.

"Fucking True. If this is the way he wants to run his club, he best be ready for a fucking blood bath."

Can't say I disagree. True crossed the line, going after Death's sister and holding Oubliette. I won't mention it if Death doesn't. If the girls haven't spoken about it, it's not mine to start a fire with.

"How is he?" I ask, sincerely concerned for Curse.

Grinding his teeth, he steps close. "Did you have anything to do with it, Busta?"

Calmly, I uncross my own arms and relax slightly. Death's stance is on guard but deflating as I answer, "Nah. I wasn't involved."

He's a big guy too, just like me. At almost six four, black hair—long and tied back at the nape—his native heritage is apparent. I think it would be a good fight.

Stepping down the hall until he's no more than ten feet away, he chirps, "You held my sister." He's pissed, and rightly so.

"Again, not my call."

Inspecting me for a lie, I know the moment he's satisfied with the answer. I fixed it, not fucked it. I can't tell him that or I'd blow it all. For now, vague answers will have to do.

Changing subjects, his voice is calmer. "This is a bad way for you to gain the gavel, Busta."

As I take a step forward, moving slowly, his boys take a defensive stance. Waving it off, he tells his boys to stay. They're fearful of leaving him alone, but so are mine. I turn to Flight and the others. "Stay here. I'll be fine."

Flight isn't as certain as I am. Gripping my arm, I look to his hand, and then at the man. Flight is close to my size. He's a good fighter, but not near dirty enough to take me down. My road name is Busta for a reason, and I doubt he wants to get a firsthand experience today. I'll flatten his ass with the mood I'm in.

"I don't think that's a good idea," he says with trepidation.

"Flight. Stay here."

"Pres—" he tries, then stops.

Walking away from the nervous bitch, I come face-to-face with Death. He sticks a hand out, looking for me to shake on it, to show there's no deceit.

"Swear on your cut that you've got nothing to do with what happened."

Without hesitation, I grasp it. "I had nothing to do with Curse or his family."

"You didn't stop True from going on the attack, though." His grip is tight, and his features show the anger that's seething just under the surface.

"I guess not." No use in arguing the point. He's right.

Just like with the Bows and the flesh trade, I've lied to myself that I was legit. At least more legit than the Cruel Intentions had been. That staying out of the darker parts of the Bows, I wasn't causing harm directly. Until Obi, I hadn't admitted it. I'd let it continue. I *could've* stopped it at any time.

The truth is, I'd gone through the motions because I'd had an out all along, I just didn't choose it. No one else in the Bows has been given the opportunity to choose, but now I have a chance to take the Bows legit, if just for a while. Now I just have to figure a way out of the mess with King.

Releasing my hand, he crosses his arms. "So, do we just fight it out in the hall or find a solution?"

Leaning on the opposite wall, I cross my feet and consider the best course of action. "Both of us lost membership today, so I'd say solutions are best. Don't you agree?"

"Only if you tell me the story about my sister and Oubliette. I need the air clear on that shit. Jasmine said you were the one holding them—"

"I was there. Let's just say there were complications, and that eventually they found their way to freedom." I can't say more without giving away information that he's not privy to, but it should be enough to calm his need for answers.

Pleased with that, Death nods. "We need to sort out some things. I think we need a meet." He turns his eyes toward the brothers listening in. "Alone."

Looking down the hall, past the nurse's station, I see the sign for a safe area where we can talk without interruptions. "Chapel?"

"No time like the present then." Motioning for me to lead, we walk off from our men to settle this between our clubs. A short-term truce is better than further bloodshed.

Chapter

Busta

We'd been standing in the silent rectory for ten minutes before others that were using the space cleared as two very large, very mean looking bikers in cuts waltzed in, ending their peaceful prayers.

Finally taking a seat, the pew groans under Death's weight. "You'd best believe Oubliette makes the best fucking drinks I've ever tasted, and while she acts tough as nails, something broke her."

It broke me too. He has no idea that I'd rather die than harm her, but he may figure it out.

I thought I could handle the things we do. I thought I was tough enough to turn a blind eye and continue without comment or concern. Not so. My facade has cracked, and the little blonde with defiance in her eyes is who chipped it away.

"How is she?" I truly want to know.

Leaning his head in his hands, he sits forward. "Honestly? I can't look her in the eye. I'm tortured by the strength she possesses every time I see the bandages and the hand marks. I've had a soft spot for that cute little girl ever since she walked through our door. Her long blonde hair, that hippie attire, and the fearless way she puts everyone in their place. I tell ya, I've always thought she was too sweet for our world. Definitely shocks me how she's handled all this."

Obi isn't someone I would have expected in the *'hold your own'* category, but she does. Maybe she'd make a great old lady?

Shaking off the thought, I decide to give him the truth, and how it all started with her seeing True's cold-blooded murder of his half-sister. By the time I'm done, Death's even more upset. He had no love for Crystal, but she didn't deserve the pain and agony that her own family put her through.

Standing up and pacing back and forth, he finally calms enough to speak. "That's some fucked-up trash that leads your club. If I'm being honest, I think it needs new leadership."

Finding that comment almost the same as King's, I inquire, "What's he got on you?"

Death turns to me. "Who, True? That piece of shit. He's got nothin' on me."

I stand, grinding out the only name that matters, "King."

The look that crosses his features tells me the truth faster than any answer could. He owes him something too.

He rakes a hand through his beard, as if contemplating on how to proceed: Lie, or tell the truth. "He has his fingers in a lot of pockets it seems."

Sitting back down on the pew, I recline comfortably and smile. "I think we have a common goal."

He takes a seat opposite of me. "Let's talk."

B^{usta}

We work out the logistics of our accord, coming up with an agreed upon plan of attack. Thing is, it all hinges on True. I don't know the extent of King and Death's relationship, nor does Death know mine, but we have an agreement. It's not solid, but it'll do.

When I return to the nurse's desk, the same scared little woman sits behind it. I don't bother acting nice to her. "News?"

Her fear is palpable. I can see it rolling off her. "The doctor can tell you—"

"Sweetheart, I'm not waiting for some shit in a long coat to show up and tell me the same thing you can. Give it to me straight."

She pores over her paperwork, as if it will give her a different answer. "Um...the Madox men, correct?"

Leaning over the counter, I slam a hand down on the paperwork she's shuffling about. "Bracken and Kyden Madox. M-A-D-O-X."

She shivers at my intrusion before her eyes turn upward. "Deceased."

Shocking me, I feel my breath coming faster. "Which one?"

Standing, she backs away from the counter. "I'm sorry. Neither of them survived."

"Busta," Flight says, touching my shoulder.

Pushing him off, I ask the frightened bird again, "I'm sorry. Maybe I didn't explain properly. There are twins here, the Madox men. Kyden and Bracken. You're telling me that they're both dead?" Grasping a thread of composure, I try to calm down. It's not her fault, and my patience wanes for her fearfulness. "The doctors in this fucking establishment couldn't save either of them? You couldn't save *one* of them!" Kicking the soft wood under the counter, it cracks under my attack.

"Busta!" I hear Death call out. "It's not her fault. Give her some space."

Looking at the woman that's cowering against the wall, I walk away. "Fuck!"

This is fucked up. I never intended to be the head of the table. King arranged everything in minuscule ways. Bit by fucking bit, he pushed the envelope until everything worked in his favor. I know it.

It's too much to handle all at once. Losing the leadership of our club, gaining the gavel, owing a debt to King...all for her. All because of her.

Finding the stairwell, I bust through the door, taking the stairs two at a time until I reach the main floor. Pushing through the front, I find it packed with kids, parents, folks in wheelchairs, attendants, and aged volunteers. My seething need to cause mayhem is overwhelming. With so many people around, I nearly run for the exit. Bursting through the sliding doors to the light of day, I head straight for my ride.

I can hear Flight yell out once I'm straddling my ride, but I don't care, nor do I look back. "Fuck off. I need to clear my head."

Starting it and pushing it back, I speed out of there as fast as I can.

O**ubliette**
     The day is warm, thankfully. I'm wearing loose shorts, a thin shift of a shirt—that I borrowed—and comfortable trainers. Making the way down from the clubhouse toward my condo in the downtown core, I'm loving the quiet. No one knows who I am. No one can feel bad that I've been through *that*.

No one will say sorry.

With a complete club lockdown, Humble is 'officially' under renovations, so I'm on a vacation of sorts. When I get to my place, I'm curling up with a bottle of wine, a heaping plate of cheese and crackers, and a soak in my tub until I wrinkle. I'll call Grady to tell him I'm home and safe. I still don't want to see him, as the last thing I need is his pity. My older brother Grady is an investment banker. The best thing he can do is shut down someone's accounts with an anonymous call to the feds. He's in no way considered *scary* to illegal biker gangs or the likes. He invests—not very intimidating.

Feeling I can breathe a bit easier with every step I take, I continue on in a trance toward my sanctuary. Three blocks and I'll be home. I tick it down. My sanity and safety are within reach.

Waiting at a light for it to change, transports fly by, and guys honk as I stand there, sticking their heads out with whistles and catcalls. It makes me even more self-conscious about my attire.

"Hey, baby. Come here!"

"Gorgeous, you need a ride?"

"Man, those legs! Come rest them here."

When the light finally changes, I look straight at the ground and move quickly. With my mind on the intention of getting home and nothing more, I don't notice the distinct sound of a motorcycle. The revving engine rumbles, bounding off the surrounding buildings as it comes closer. It's frightening how it makes one seem like a hundred.

"Oubliette!" the person shouts.

I ignore them, quickening my steps across the intersection.

The motorcycle quiets. "Obi!" they shout again.

Shit, I know that voice!

I want so bad to leave everything behind and regain my life. To act as if nothing ever happened.

It seems I can't.

I break into a sprint.

I want to be home.

I want to be anywhere but here.

I want it to be anyone but *him*.

Why me?

Why again?

Why now?

Running, as if the hounds of hell are on my heels, I hear the moment the Harley starts up again.

I curse my bad luck.

God dammit!

The *one* biker that I least wish to see is coming after me.

Moving as fast as I can, with my throat and lungs burning from the pain, I push through it. I remind myself that I escaped the first time and I need to again. I won't be taken again.

All I can do is find a way around this.

I can. I know I can. I think I can.

That's when Busta's Harley jumps the curb directly in front of me. With a cocky grin and a gun raised, the dangerous Busta halts my escape.

He turns off his bike. "Obi, I'm not playing. This isn't a game, sweetheart. Stop."

Falling to my knees, I scuff my hands on the pavement. "Please. I can't go back there. Please let me go, Busta. I can't...I just can't," I plead with every ounce of my soul. There's no way I'd survive that place again. I'd die first before setting foot inside there again.

"I'm not taking you there, Obi. I promise." Putting his gun down, he raises his other hand, which holds his phone. "Here, call Death, he'll confirm it."

I don't understand. "What? Why?"

"He can explain it, or you can trust me and let me explain it to you. Your choice." Popping the kickstand on his bike, he rises and steps toward me. "Here, I'll dial."

Dialing a number, he then puts it on speaker. With each ring, I wonder if he's telling the truth.

Until I hear Bennett answer. "Busta? What's up, man?"

"Death, I happened upon someone in your care down the street. She wants to hear it from you that I wish her no harm." He turns the phone my way. "Go ahead, Obi."

"Bennett?" I ask.

"Oubliette? What the hell are you doing out of the compound? Never mind that. Tell me you're okay."

"Yeah, I'm okay. Should I trust him?" I look up at Busta. His dark scowl has softened, and I catch him inspecting my bandages. Turning his head back and forth, his scowl deepens every time he sees something he's unhappy with.

"We have an understanding. He'll keep you safe, Oubliette. Stay with him, please. If I know you're safe, I can concentrate on other things." Bennett's voice is calm as he tells me this, so I trust he's leaving me in good hands. "Oh, and Oubliette? I'll let Jasmine know you're safe. I'm guessing she doesn't know you're off walking the town."

I wince. He's right. She'll be pissed. "No, she doesn't. Only Apoc and Malice saw me leave."

"I'll be having words with them. Hey, Busta?"

Tearing Busta's attention away from my wounds, he answers Bennett. "Yeah, brother?"

"Don't let her out of your sight." With that, Bennett hangs up.

Pocketing his phone, Busta smiles. It's handsome on him. I still don't trust him, but if Bennett feels he's a safer bet than me wandering alone, I'll give in. For now.

Hopping across his ride, he grabs up a helmet and holds it out to me. "Your ride, my lady."

"You think I'll just jump on a bike with you, even with Bennett's blessing?"

"Well, if you'd like, you can run beside it. On the highway, it could be a bit scary."

Taking the helmet, I place it on my head and fasten the latch. "I've never been on a bike."

He nods. "Step on here, sling your leg over, then place your foot on the peg on the other side."

I've seen others ride, obviously, but I've never done it myself.

Tucking my hair down the back of my shirt and resting my ass behind Busta on the tiny seat, I ready myself mentally to ride behind him. I know I need to hang on, but the last place I want my hands are around him. Being this close is terrifying. Not because he's scary, but because I know where I have to put my hands. Our relationship so far hasn't been the most cordial. I'd rather take that gun of his and hold it to his temple.

"Come on, Obi. Put your arms around me." Grasping one of my hands, he pulls it around his waist. "The last thing I want is for you to get hurt further."

Blowing out a heavy breath, I resign myself to the situation. In this position, my breasts are pressed against his back, my hands are dangerously close to his belt line, and I can feel the perfected abs of his stomach.

"Hold on."

Starting the bike and turning up the street, we tear off. I don't know where we're going, but it's decidedly the wrong direction for me.

I *wanted* to go home, and as I see it shrink into the background over my shoulder, I watch the surroundings.

If I need to escape him again, it's better to know where I am.

Hopefully, I won't have to.

B<u>usta</u>

After our little chat, Death and I agreed to work as one unit. We noticed there were major similarities in our club *issues*.

King. The genius behind our strife.

It's *always* been King.

Our clubs are players on his chessboard. No more. Thing is, we've realized he's a dirty motherfucker, and that he's profiting off of all the ventures he's got his fingers in.

Lots of pies, lots of little ventures.

He was hedging his bets that we'd never get along or find a common goal. We have one now. That's why Oubliette wandering the streets on her own is dangerously naive. She's worked at Humble, completely oblivious to the shitshow. King is in with the Army. Who knows? Maybe he's even in with the Bastards, the SoCal Soulless, and the Alta Noche too.

King is ruining the life she knew, the one she can't go back to.

So that brings us to now. I can't take her back to the Army compound without taking a bullet to the head for the effort, and I won't go back to the Bows with her either. I know there's a mole in my camp, just as Death knows there's one in his. We need to weed them out. Being a target won't do Oubliette any good. She'll be caught in the crossfire. Whoever the mole is, they've seen Oubliette for the past five years and know the connection she has to Death and Jasmine. She's a pawn to be leveraged. Having her at the Bows clubhouse? As soon as I walk through those doors with her under my protection, that will put her on the radar there. That leaves my house. It's the safest place.

As we ride down the road, I start sussing out the bad weed in the Bows. One thing I know is that they were either at church, or have the ear of someone who was. They know I was appointed to VP from a closed room meeting, and they passed that info to King swiftly.

Stopping at another light, I check on Obi. "You good back there?" I ask over the sound of the roaring engine.

Breathing close to my ear, pushing her perfect fucking tits into my back, her sweet voice carries all the way to my core. "Yeah. So far."

"We won't be long," I shout over my shoulder. "I've got a place just outside the city limits."

Feeling her shake her head, she rests back against me. Fuck, this is going to be harder than I thought. Her on my bike was a necessity, but her sweet body pressed against mine, her hands wrapped around my waist, and her dangerously close to my dick is an itch I can't scratch.

I'm gonna need a cold shower.

Maybe more than one...

O ubliette

For the first time on a bike, it wasn't altogether terrible.

Heading down roads littered with expensive lakeland homes, making a left and turning to the water, he pulls down a driveway that stops in front of a three-car garage, red brick home.

He taps me on the leg. "Hold on for a second." Reaching into the saddlebag by my left leg, he plucks out a remote. Clicking it, the middle garage door opens. Pulling in and closing it after we park, the bike goes silent. The space is spotless. There's a gym setup out here, and a nice truck parked in the far slot. Meticulously clean.

"How you doin' after your first ride?"

My body still rumbles as I step onto the concrete floor. "It wasn't awful." If I'm being honest with myself, I actually enjoyed the freedom that his motorcycle offered. Sure, riding behind and letting another have control of my fate was weird, but I found it relaxing.

"You look like you could use a beer." Popping the door to the inside of the house, Busta holds it open for me to progress ahead of him.

Chivalrous.

Taking the offered courtesy, I wander inside. Stopping short as soon as I do, I'm floored by the interior. Banks of windows that face a crystal lake. Colorful boats travelling by. It's serene. Walking past me, Busta heads to the kitchen area. "So, you want that beer, Obi? Or something a bit stronger?"

"Whiskey. Neat," I say rather curtly, adding, "Please."

The kitchen is plain, unadorned, simplistic. Black appliances, stainless steel counter, and white cupboards.

He sets two glasses on the counter. "Not what you were expecting I suppose. Thought I'd have a room in the clubhouse? That I lived, breathed, and bled colors of the club?"

"Something like that."

While he's pouring two neat glasses, I pull out a stool and have a seat at the end. Sliding a glass across, I down it. The fire aches in my throat, but it's not bad. Shuttling the glass back to him, Busta refills it.

"So, will you tell me what's going on? Why are you and Death chummy chummy, or should I just make up the story and hope I have it right?"

Pouring himself another shot, he shrugs. "You can make up your own story, but I'm sure it won't be anywhere near the truth." Downing his glassful and refilling it, he too winces at the burn. "Nothing is near enough to the truth. Even I don't believe it."

"Start at the beginning. Go from there."

"Fair enough." Pouring another—the third—this time to the brim, his dark, steamy voice buzzes through me. I haven't eaten. I have a high tolerance for alcohol, but on an empty stomach, it won't take much to have me teetering.

"I doubt you can scare me. Lay it on me." Wincing as the sharp liquid travels past the tenderness, I hold my breath. "That shit burns."

Taking a large gulp of his own, Busta smirks. That smile is dangerous. It makes him less intimidating.

"Let's agree to disagree. I'm sure what I know will cause you to run screaming." With a hint of mischief, a dash of darkness, and a full helping of panty-melting, he grins between his well-trimmed beard. I've never really been into bearded guys, but it suits him. Add on that deep timbre voice of his, and I want to grade him on a scale like an Olympic diver.

Staring him down, I grab up my glass and gulp a few mouthfuls. I slow blink.

At this rate, I think drunk could be dangerous. I need to think of him as the enemy, not as sexy man candy. He's dark, forbidden, and crass. What I love to find in a guy and exactly wrong in all ways.

Letting out a weak cough, I rub my throat through the bandages. "Okay." Smacking the counter, trying to lighten the mood, I attempt to take the attention away from my neck. "Give it to me straight, Busta."

"Lucius," he growls. "Call me Lucius. Busta is in the clubhouse. In this house, I'm Lucius."

"Okay, *Lucius*," I return stoically. At two hundred plus in size, I've only seen the man smile twice, and his demeanor doesn't scream *Lucius*. Lucius will take a bit for me to adjust to.

"You saw True kill Crystal, right?" Kicking me out of my musings, his tone is serious.

"Yeah. Not one of my favorite moments at work."

"That's what put you in our path."

"Well, I want out of your path then," I quip back.

He leans over the counter. "That's not your choice anymore, Obi."

I scowl. I feel like I'm back in the cage squaring off with him about my name. That's the last time I'll let him get away with calling me Obi. "Oubliette. Say it, Busta. I'm not a biker with a nickname you can use. I'm not your best friend, wife, or club girl. I'm wrapped up in something I don't want to be in, and that doesn't offer up the allowance for you to call me by anything but my real name." Picking up my glass, mock cheering him, I smile condescendingly. "Got it, *Lucius*."

Smiling again, that bright grin is electric, and really quite pretty on him. "This will be fun, Obi."

He's trying to get a rise out of me. Asshole.

Staying silent, I lift my glass. At this rate, I'll be loaded in twenty minutes.

Honestly. I. Don't. Care.

I'm not locked in, I can escape, and even if I don't quite know where I am, I do know how to get back to where I was.

As I stay quiet, he tips his glass back. "Fine," he growls, swallowing the remainder of his glass.

"Fine," I retort, trying to look anywhere but his electric eyes. Instead, I stare off into the yard that overlooks the water.

While he rests back on his stool, he continues. "True killed her, and he couldn't have you telling anyone. You could've put him in a bad position with the club. That wasn't about to happen, not while he was trying to gain the gavel. You knew enough of what she was doing at Humble to be dangerous, Oubliette."

Wow. He called me by my full name. It actually disappoints me that he did. Now that I hear it, it sounds wrong.

"What if I wouldn't have said or did anything? What if I'd promised—"

"You couldn't have promised that. That's why he took you. And I'm—"

With a hand up, I halt him before he apologizes. "Let's not rehash the warehouse. I don't want to talk about it." I don't want to talk about it ever again. "Tell me then, why are you and Death getting along? 'Cause I don't see how that happens, especially after you held his sister."

Dragging my fingers through my hair and plying it into a braid, I lay it across my shoulder. I didn't have a chance to grab a wrap or elastic, and as we drove it was tangling around me. Now as we're talking about my captivity, I feel strangled by it. I need it off me. "Why did you bring me here?" I ask.

Scrunching up his brows, he asks, "What do you mean?"

"Why here? Why not take me back to the Army clubhouse, or my house? You could've gotten me out of your life. Why here, Busta?"

"Lucius," he growls again. "You're here because I can't drive to Death's clubhouse with a Bows rocker." He grasps his cut and tugs it. "I'd be shot coming around the curb. And Obi, I can't leave you in the hopes that all goes well. I won't take you to your house—"

"Condo," I correct.

"Condo then. Excuse me, Princess. I won't take you to your tower." Stepping around the counter, moving so close that his body is now touching mine, I feel the heat, the power that courses through him. I see the faint scars that peek out from under his beard, and the dark freckles that until you're really up close, you don't see in his dark skin. I don't want to say that I haven't been attracted to him, because I have been from the start.

Lucius is the wrong man to be attracted to.

With him so close, I have an urgent need to escape before I do something stupid. "Which way is the bathroom?" I ask, standing quickly from my stool.

"On the right." He points down the hall.

Rushing inside and closing the door, I grab a towel and wet it. Patting my face, I try to calm my already tortured thoughts and buzzing body from the attraction I have to him. I consider the consequences. Not because he's a biker, and not because he's a very large man that scares me. Nope. None of that. He's dangerous because I could fall for him. He's the type of man I'm attracted to whether I'll admit it or not. I want the strong, silent, resilient, caring, dependable, and would kill on sight if I was harmed kind of man. He's my kind of dangerous.

It's like Beauty and the Beast. He's the *Beast*. He's broken, tortured, and dangerous enough to scare me away, but not enough to stop me from seeing there's room for redemption. I was the captive, just like Belle.

And now I'm in his castle. Now I'm held against my will.

How do I get out of this? The answer: I can't. I'm stuck wanting him, needing to know more, to find out if the man I think that's beneath *is*.

I can't shake off the smell of him, the nearness, the desperate need to feel those lips pressed to mine. Pulling in a deep, sharp breath, harsh enough it stings, I head back out. It could be the biggest mistake of my life, but the driving need is too hard to resist.

Chapter

O ubliette
I have to ask the burning question sticking in my head, the one kicker that could ruin that need to feel his lips.

Stepping in, arms crossed, I ask, "Tell me one thing, and I need complete honesty." My voice still sounds so crackly. The words stick and break. The compression from Nock hopefully hasn't caused long-term damage. It's still uncomfortable. But this question is so important, I push past the pain.

"Shoot."

"Did you put me in the cage to teach me a lesson?"

His silence tells the truth. Stepping close, coming within my space, Lucius growls out, "For only a second. Maybe two, Oubliette."

I stand still, shocked.

Grasping his drink and offering me mine, I take the cup. "Nock's arrival sealed my incarceration. Great."

"Yeah, it did."

The tension as we stand within each other's space is palpable.

Reaching for my hand, the one holding the cup, Lucius brings me close. We're separated only by our clothing. "That place is a nightmare."

Laughing lightly, pulling my drink to my lips, I mumble, "I can't disagree."

"You don't get it. I swore to the club I'd never step foot in that place. Calling me in to look after you, they knew...they knew it was the last place I wanted to be." He sounds apologetic.

I *almost* believe him.

With only mere inches separating us, and my glass empty, I'm fearful. I'm anticipating the contact. It's been a long time coming. At least I've dreamt it.

In my own defense, I was delirious from a lack of oxygen. I'd had an attempt on my life.

That was only a few days ago.

This is so wrong. So, so wrong.

I need to stop all thoughts of him, which is frustratingly difficult with the smell, look, and need to taste him. I'm warring with my own libido.

"Obi," he sighs. He's trying his own resolve. He's calling me by my nickname, hoping it will deter me and remind me that I should hate him, despise him—see him as the enemy. I don't, though. I only see the broken, the damaged, the redeemable.

Placing a finger on his soft lips, I trace them. They're supple, full, and they're bitable. Exactly as I thought. His breath is relaxed as I smooth my finger along the seam. The tough exterior of this hardened biker falls away as he accepts my touch.

"Obi..." He turns his eyes away from me.

Bringing his sights back my way, I whisper, "Lucius. Don't stop me."

Wrapping a hand in his hair, tugging on him to give me what I want, I feel him denying our attraction. It's been there from the beginning, and I won't ignore it any longer. The pain in my core as I consider him, the ache in my heart as I see what he's capable of—I want it all. His torture, his solitude.

I want to see all of him.

Leaning forward, gliding my tongue across his lips, I notice the tension dissipate as his own reaches out to caress mine. Wrestling his tongue against mine, finally he gives me what I ask for—his all. As our heavy breaths combine, he tangles a hand in my braid and holds it tight. I wrap a free arm around his chest—or at least as far as I can. As I push my body tight to his, he groans within my mouth. I love it.

Tugging my braid tighter, pulling my head back slightly, our mouths come apart. "Fuck. The shit I've thought about doing to you, Obi."

"It isn't far off of what I hope for I'll bet," I reply with a smile.

"Don't say that." Releasing the braid, letting it fall, he steps back an inch. "Don't ask for something you don't know the outcome to."

I grasp his cut and pull him close. "I didn't have an expectation, but I do hope for something close to the dream."

He narrows his eyes. "And that would be?"

"That *you're* not a dream." My voice sounds pleading and greedy—I know it does, but my head knows what it wants. Reaching down between us, feeling the engorged cock that strains against his jeans, I actually have a sudden sense of fear. It's more than I expected.

He gives me a wicked grin. "More man than you've had?" Laying his hand on mine, he tightens his grip, forcing me to feel the full width.

"Lucius."

Saying his name garners a bigger smile. "I like the sound of my name on your lips. I think I'd like it screamed out loud better." Dragging his hands under my ass, he tips me toward him, resting me aloft his waist. Pressing his mouth tight to mine, his tongue is commanding and hungry. Holding me tight to his body, we traverse down the hall. Hitting the edge of a doorframe, bounding into the space, he lays me on the end of the bed. "I'm gonna make you scream so much, your voice will be hoarse."

Looking down at my bandage, his eyes widen and he curses. Rising off the bed, Lucius proceeds to walk out of the room, but pauses in the doorway. "Get some rest, Oubliette."

Shutting the door and walking away, I hear his boots clack down the hall. I'm so surprised by his turnabout that I'm speechless as he leaves.

What the fuck was that?

Busta

I'm an asshole.

I'm an epic asshole of shit-stick proportions.

My mind is so sexually clouded with the prospect of having Oubliette under me that I'd so easily forgotten what she's been through, what she's endured.

She *is* strong.

Looking down on her, reminding myself that she'd gone through more than most, I think anyone other than her would've crashed and burned, broken into pieces and asked for the wreckage to be spread to the four corners of the Earth.

Not her, though.

I'd almost forgotten.

Because my dick said so.

Because *she* said so.

Her body called to me. I knew it was wrong. Not because she's hurt, but because she's protected by the Army—by Death and his boys. I gave him my word she'd be protected.

That means from me.

That means even from *herself.*

She needs to stay far away from me. Her sweetness can't be tainted by me and my past failures. I'd failed my family. I swear I won't fail her.

Tucking my aching cock to the side, I consider having a shower to rub it out to release the tension. It's the last thing I want, but it's probably for the best. Walking out to the kitchen for another whiskey, I pour glass after glass, sucking back on the fiery taste until my senses dull, reveling in the solitude.

Ending at the fifth glassful, I place it in the dishwasher and work at keeping my wits about me. I won't be able to protect a container of strawberries from a butterfly if I'm drunk.

She's too important to lose.

I blame myself for everything that happened while she was in my care at the warehouse. I blame myself for not stopping Nock. And yeah, I blame myself *for* Nock's death. I blame myself for letting him taunt her, and for laughing it off too. I thought, 'What harm could come of leaving her in there?' I was so fucking wrong.

Touching her now would be wrong.

Under no circumstances will she change my mind.

Oubliette and I will *never* get together.

Chapter

Oubliette

I'm destined to fight in this war. Flopping on the bed, wanton and in need, I'm nothing more than a clustered ball of lust. Because of *him*. No, it's because of me. He wants what I want, I know it, but being reminded of my damaged throat and the pain that Nock put me through, he decided it was best to leave me wanting.

Well, fuck him!

Screw this!

I'll leave *him* in need.

Rising off the bed, tearing down the flimsy shorts and tossing them across the room, I pull the bedding back. The down cover is strewn on the floor haphazardly, and the soft cotton sheets beckon me.

Walking to the door and pulling it back open, I make sure it's wide enough for him to hear, and see, what he's missing.

Lying back on the bed, I imagine his mouth trailing down my skin. My body instantly reacts as I touch the areas I know causes the deepest tingles. Tweaking a nipple here, laying light touches across my hip bones, I pad across my skin to my core. Splaying my legs slightly, thumbing the skin to part, I toy with my body. I don't do it quietly either. It still aches to hum and moan, but I enjoy every ounce of what I know feels amazing. What I know he'll hear as I bring myself to release.

As I feel my bud rising, I taunt myself more and more. I don't want it to end easily, and I don't want it over too quickly. I want him to want it. To feel it.

Enraptured in my own care, I don't notice him until he arrives and stands by the door. Looking to him will give away the ruse, so I turn away from him and look to the window. I know he's there, but it doesn't matter. He needs to break.

Stroking faster, I feel as my excitement crests. I won't last much longer, but that's fine. He's here now. "Lucius, mmm..." Calling his name, I wiggle on the bed. "Oh my God, that's it. It's wonderful right there." Accentuating my verbalization of excitement, I act it up a tad because I'm not letting up until he breaks.

"Suck it, please. Please make the sting go away." Writhing on the bed, coming near my end, I'm pushing myself to the edge of despair. Waiting for him to crack, I hear the door to the room slam against the wall.

"Fuck," is all he says before shoving my hands out of the way to finish what I'd started. On his knees, dragging me to the edge of the bed, his mouth is perfection as it dances across the surface. Pulling the end of my need from me, I yell out in earnest.

The ache deepens until I explode with a painful, throaty growl, "Lucius!"

I scream dark and deep. It hurts, but it's more than amazing at the same time. It's everything I could've expected. His large hands holding my body down as I raise my hips toward him. His mouth covering me and plying everything from me—every last drop of my demise. That's when I know I'm well and fucked. I've given everything to Lucius and I can't go back.

I need all of him. Every piece of him.

The Hade's Army be damned. The Broken Bows too.

When Lucius tosses his cut to the discarded duvet, his tee and jeans follow suit shortly after. Through my post release bliss, I vaguely see him gather a condom from a bedside table.

"You wanted me. You taunted me for what you want. If you scream and hurt yourself further in the process, know that I'm stopping, Obi."

"I'll be quiet."

Creeping up the bed, stalking until he reaches where I lie, he covers my body with his. Kissing me deeply, I taste myself on him. I've never had that before, and in a way, it drives me to want more. "Obi, I'll be as gentle as I can, but I'm not a gentleman." As his dark eyes pierce into mine, I know that he can't deny his need.

Pulling his bearded chin, kissing his lips again, I smile. "I'm not a fragile flower, Lucius."

'No, you're not." He enters me. He's so big that my body rebels.

Groaning, he pushes within. "Jesus, fuck!"

"I agree." I've never been a talker during sex, but Lucius makes me want to be. Though I've promised to be quiet, I have the distinct feeling I'll break that promise quickly.

Rising to meet his hips, I feel when he's fully inside. It's painful, but in a beautiful way. Rising and lowering with his strokes, I love the feel. The firm tightening of my muscles as they contract toward another release is perfection. I won't last long at this rate, but I don't care.

He pulls my body back. "I'm going to come if you squeeze like that, Obi," he grinds out. Lifting my body off the bed, rising with a strength I knew he possessed, he holds my body tight to his. Standing, resting me against the wall, he pumps his hips upward. With my legs wrapped around him, he pounds into me for all he's worth.

I try to hold it in, but it's so hard. I make tiny noises, holding in the majority of them because I swore I would. My breathing becomes raspy and short.

Rather loudly, I shout, "More! I want more!"

Bowing my back off the wall, soaking up his powerful strokes, I come again. This time it's so strong, I feel every bone in my body vibrate from the aftershocks. Lucius doesn't stop, though. Continuing even as every muscle of mine tightens to a point of pushing him out, he holds my body hostage. I feel as if I've been ran down by a Mack truck.

Every inch screams.

Every nerve sings its joy.

Every one of the tiny neurons in my mind say *yes, yes, yes! Encore!* But I don't think I could take another moment of it...yet.

A twenty-minute recoup could be necessary.

He kisses my forehead. "Wow," is all he says as he backs my body off the wall. Taking me to the bed, splaying me out sweetly, I howl at the lack of fullness within me. That gains me a laugh. A real laugh. Something I wasn't sure he was capable of.

"I'll be right back." Rising from the bed he heads to a bathroom, and returns a few moments later with a fresh towel. Then going to his closet, he pulls out a shirt, a pair of boxers and a sweater. "Here. The shower's finicky, and the soap smells like a man. But at least you'll feel refreshed." He turns to gather his things from the floor. "I'll go make us something to eat while you do."

Leaving me with a smile, Lucius walks away.

Tossing my head back, my exhausted body reminds me of how that felt. Everything is noticing a tenderness—but in a good way.

Smirking, I take off for the shower.

B<u>usta</u>

I almost couldn't believe what I was seeing.

The little minx had left the door open on purpose, setting me up for failure. There was no way of winning that game. As soon as I saw her fingers pulling back those sweet lips, I was crushed. Out of a stupid loyalty to the clubs I was leaving her alone, but fuck them.

She's a grown woman and I'm a grown ass man. I was taking what she was offering.

And when I fucked her, I had no way to return from that. I'd laughed at the guys back at the club when they were so dick whipped they couldn't even piss without asking—all because of a woman's cunt. I had no value in that. But the payoff of her and what she did, I'd gamble my ass on a whip. And carnally sinking myself between her legs? I've never done that with the whores. They're too diseased to consider it. Obi tastes like a sweet peach, and I'll for sure do that again.

I left her in my bedroom with a Bow's T-shirt and one of my favorite band sweaters—the best white guy to sound like a brother. I can't wait to see her walk through the kitchen with it on. Honestly, it's really in my best interest to clothe the woman.

My place isn't cold by any means, but it is cool. I'm sure she'll make mention of it. I don't adjust the temp as it's perfect all year round, and the last thing I need to see through a threadbare white tee is her sweet budded nipples. I'd never eat a real meal again. She'd be my buffet.

Taking bacon and eggs from the fridge, I get to work on feeding us. Oubliette is my first house guest. If I have a choice, she'll be the only one *ever*.

Getting to work on our food, I hear her start the shower. When my phone buzzes across the counter beside me, I turn it over. My smile dissipates and my frown returns.

Motherfucker.

"Yeah. Go."

"Where are you, Pres?" Smart asks.

Not sure I'm gonna get used to that.

"Out. Why? You need a diaper change?" I'm pissy, but it's not his fault. He has no idea he's ruining my high.

"Well, we were out looking for Scarlet and I think we found her." That doesn't sound good at all.

"Yeah? Where?" I grind out as I crack two eggs into a bowl.

His voice is tentative. "She's being walked out of the police station with guys in DEA jackets surrounding her."

Tossing an egg at the window, I curse out loud. "What the fuck'd you say?"

"I'm sitting across the street on my bike watching her. I see her clear as day, walking in cuffs with three DEA motherfuckers."

With my rage simmering under the surface, I try to beat the eggs in the bowl instead of smashing more against the wall. "Tell me."

Explaining King down to the shiny brown loafers the fucker loves to wear, he and his pinhead asshole sidekicks lead Scarlet to a black van. When he's done and the van is pulling away, I tell him to follow the fuckers. I want more info when he has it. As I hang up the line, frustrated and annoyed, I realize my frustration isn't with him—it's King.

Setting my phone on the counter, still seething, I step down the hall. Knocking on the door to the bathroom, I yell in, "I'm going out to the garage for a moment."

"I'll be out soon!"

"No rush," I say as I start away.

Smacking the remote for the door, it rises slowly, allowing light in. Light or not, I need to pound on the heavy bag to reduce my stress. Pelting into the side of it, imagining it's King's face, I punch it over and over.

I think about all the things he's done to *my* life. If it weren't for King, I'd have my family, my parents, and my club. Instead, I have a presidency that *shouldn't* have been mine. I'd always thought I would be a member of the Cruel Intentions. I'd grown up *wanting* that. My skin itches where my Bows tattoo rests—a daily reminder that it should be three reapers with crossed swords.

I can't go back now, that club is gone. That family's scattered and a part of someone else's life—of Lucius Gueirra's life. One with my brother, my sister and a club I adored. Pounding on the bag as if it owes me something, I push those thoughts away. I can't be that man. I can deal with the now.

Continuing to slam my fists into the bag, I think of how someone like Obi shouldn't have been subjected to what she was. That she should be living a life where she's fucking the nice guy—the good guy. Not me. She shouldn't be here. Not for a moment, not for a second. Our life, our club, and the danger that flesh trafficking brought to her door isn't something she should've even known existed.

If I had a choice, I'd rather not have known it existed either.

Swinging my fists, my muscles work to the point of weakening. It feels right. The pressure that mounts on my shoulders feels like my body can't hold up the needs of others anymore.

This is all on True. Fucker had to use his sister as a spy in the Army, instead of letting us work it out the right way. Killing her caused this whole fucking mess. A mess, that as pres, is now mine.

Mine.

Now I'm president—the *king*. True and DG left behind dangerous business dealings I had no care to inherit.

No more.

No more will I be a part of that.

No more will the Bows.

No more young girls and women. *Hit, hit.*

No more dealing with the cartel.

No more drugs and mules. *Hit, hit.*

No more infighting with the other clubs. *Hit, hit.*

No more.

I don't want us in the seedy shit. The Broken Bows will be legit. I'll possibly have a fight on my hands from the guys, but I'll make this club right.

We're taking ourselves off the market for the DEA.

And Magnus King? I'm taking him down. If he thinks he'll fuck me over for it, he'll pay. I have enough on him and his dirty workings that he'll never survive.

The man may be a cockroach, but I'm about to stomp him out.

Oubliette

After a steaming shower, I towel dried my hair as much as possible. Plaiting it to the side and peering at myself in the foggy mirror, the bruises are nearly nonexistent. The scars are internal. To me, I see his fingers, I see his face, I see his wide eyes.

Those eyes are imprinted on the back of my lids every time I close them. I've tried to keep awake to block him out, but even in my waking mind, Nock's glare shocks me.

Flicking the light off and leaving the fan running, I leave the room.

Deciding to check out the house, as Lucius is in the garage, I take a tour. It's not massive, but it's comfortable in its entirety. There are two bedrooms—one that looks like it's never been touched—an office that's empty, a laundry room and the kitchen. That's it, other than the living room I'm standing in. There's great light in here. Any artist would be in heaven. Or a cat. Cat's love light. Heck, my brother's big dog would love this space.

Me? I notice the sophistication of nothing. Empty is beautiful. My condo is similar. I know guys think girls are clutterbugs, but I love simplicity.

Seeing a mess on the window and egg shells on the floor, I have to say I'm surprised. For a man who seems regimented, stark, and particular in his surroundings, an egg on the window is out of place. Grabbing a cloth and spray from the kitchen, I clean it up.

While I do, I hear Lucius in the garage. There's smacking, banging, thumping, and grunting—he seems pretty pissed. I think it's best if I leave him a bit longer.

On the counter, there's a few eggs in a container, half beaten in a bowl, bread, and a package of bacon. I might as well finish what he'd started. Cooking up the eggs and bacon, I get to work on the toast while it fries up.

At some point, I couldn't handle hearing Lucius' melodic pounding further, so I turned on the stereo. Cranking the volume, music I didn't expect blasts from the speakers. Old-school rap makes the windows rattle.

"Shit!" Scrambling across the room to the receiver, I turn down the volume as fast as I can. Once it's at a rate tolerable, I start back on the food.

Moving with the beat, I enjoy music that I haven't heard in a while. The food smells amazing, causing my rapidly starving stomach to grumble.

Walking to the garage door, hoping that he's exhausted and starved enough that I won't be a target, I decide that there are other ways to distract him—just in case. Pulling the sweater off, wearing only the white Broken Bows tee he gave me, my nipples are noticeable through the material.

With a deep breath, I open the door and watch him, the way he shifts, moves, and throws all his energy into a punch. I'm amazed by the strong man killing a heavy bag.

Deciding it's best to inject humor into the moment, I say, "If you have that much energy, I can give you other things to do rather than kill a poor defenseless bag."

Looking me in the eyes, his fire dissipates. His dark skin has a sheen to it from the sweat, his soft soulful eyes are strong and direct. "Where's the sweater I gave you?"

His body is drenched in sweat, the shirt stuck to the plains of his chest, perfectly showcasing his strong body.

"Inside." I indicate with a quirk of my head. "How long do you feel like killing that?" Crossing my ankles and leaning on the doorframe, his smile-free face searches mine. His expression lights up the room. It's easy to see that this garage—this workout room, has never had a woman in it. It's built for one purpose. Not a car, not a bike, which is parked on the other side. Nope. This room is for clearing out the cobwebs in your head.

He wipes his face down with a towel. "How long have I been out here?"

"Long enough." Smiling wide, I don't dare tell him he's been out here for over an hour. "But you still seem to have a ton of energy to expel." Tapping the button for the garage, I giggle as it closes. "I'm hungry, and someone promised me a meal."

Seeming sort of sorry for that, he smirks and steps up to me. "I didn't mean to be gone that long." It's a nearly nonexistent smile, but I can see his beard twitch. "Let me feed you, woman."

Reaching out, he tweaks my nipple. Squealing slightly, I pull in a lungful of air as he grips my boob tight. He's so intense, it's crazy.

I've gone from being the captive—I've said it before—to a captive on my own terms. I'm here because I *want* to be. This isn't by someone else's rules. This is different.

But is it different for him I wonder?

Chapter

B usta

I'm drenched, worn-out, and annoyed by King, but that's not her issue. Deflating my anger, rolling my shoulders and tossing the towel to the side as she walks out, I pull the wrappings off my hands.

Standing there, wearing only my white tee that shows everything, I'm amiss. Her pert nipples call to me. They ask to be molested—to be used and abused. Seeing those soft, imploring, and questioning eyes, it changes my need to destroy, use, and abuse. I wish to make her smile.

As I pull at her needy nipple through the white tee, she doesn't move. Covering her pillowy tit in my hand, her little intake of breath increases my need to pull her apart all over again. But then I catch a whiff of myself. Sweat is not sexy.

"Oubliette, I smell awful. I need a shower."

"Hmm. A conundrum." She smirks, training her eyes low. Gripping my shirt, she attempts to pull me closer.

I stay put.

Smelling her fresh from the shower, feeling her body heat close, I toy with the loose hair that loops near her ear. My blood screams in my ears as my cock engages its interest once more. Looping an arm under her ass and lifting her over my shoulder, I pop open the door from the garage to the house. Wandering in, music blasts me.

"Rap, huh?"

From over my shoulder, she pipes up, "Well, I didn't search through your playlists, and I'm good with this."

Setting Obi on the leather couch with a skin-slapping thunk, her naked pussy flies through the air. Momentarily it distracts me. Who am I kidding? Seeing it is more than a momentary distraction.

Hopping over the back of the couch, I push her knees apart and smile. "I'm hungry."

Her breath hitches. "Well I cooked."

"Not what I want to eat, Obi."

Staring down at that sweet center, it calls to me. Like a starved man, I sink myself between her folds. Mewling and sighing, Obi grinds her hips upward to meet my mouth. Her scent, her taste—I won't quit until she comes at least twice, then I'm sinking myself deep. Finding a particularly sensitive point on her body, I hold myself to trace it exclusively until she breaks.

Obi's release is addictive.

"Lucius!"

Christ, even that's something I could enjoy hearing on a daily basis. Her gravelly voice—in a dangerous and sadistic way, in a greedy way, I hope she keeps it. Yeah, I'm an asshole for thinking that, but I love the sound of her mewling underneath me. How her growl turns me on further.

Rising, tossing off my tee and throwing down my jeans, I seat myself within her. To hear her fall apart again so quickly, nothing else matters. I want every squeeze, sound, cry and scratch as she grips my body.

"Deeper, deeper!" she screams out with her fingers digging into my ass. Pulling me tight to her, I thrust harder. The way her body responds is perfection. After one moment, my body has become addicted to the feel of her heat. Rocking harder, holding her hips as handles, I move faster and faster, doing as she asks until my body releases the tension I've held in. If I thought I was sweaty before, I'm dripping as I toss all the power left within me into my movements.

Grasping me like a vise, Obi cries out as her climax stiffens her whole body. That's when that's it for me. Thrusting one last time, I come within her as if my life depends on it.

"Holy shit, that was better than the last round, Lucius." Smiling, she lies back, sated.

I feel the same.

Sated.

Backing out of her body, I wince as her tight walls try to hold me in.

Oh, shit.

"Christ, Obi. I wasn't thinking. I didn't put on a condom." That's a first for me.

Pushing herself up on her elbows, the shock on her face undoubtedly mirrors mine. "That's unfortunate. Please tell me you're clean. It won't make it perfect, but better."

"Yeah. No whore's touched this without a layer." It may seem casual to say, but it's true. Not one has. I've always been careful. Then again, I've never lost my head in a woman's body.

Lifting off the couch, squeaking out from underneath, Obi grins, then kisses my lips sweetly. "I'm taking another shower."

"I'm joining."

"What if I don't want you there?"

Lifting her up to stand, I laugh. "Not giving you a choice, sweetheart."

Pulling down the tee until it hits her knees, Obi grips a bare nipple of mine and yanks it, causing me to bend down toward her. "I have a choice. But I choose to have you there, Lucius. Remember that."

Petting her head, with her sweet blonde sex hair sticking up, I kiss her sweetly on the forehead. "Remembered."

Pointing to my beard as she walks away, her little fairy growl chimes out, "You have a little something there."

Chapter

B<u>usta</u>

The outcome of this can have repercussions in my life for a long time to come. I came inside her. Fuck. I've never been so foolish.

Hitting the floor of the bathroom for the second time in less than two hours, she strips off the borrowed tee. Starting the water, bent over, pulling up the diverter, I stand behind her, inspecting that perfect ass.

Turning tail down the hall behind her with a fresh erection starting, I resign myself to the idea that she's mine. I don't care how, or how long it takes, but Oubliette will be mine for good.

Fuck. If I'd ever heard one of the boys talking like that, I'd have busted their balls for weeks.

Fuck it. I'm Pres now, right? It's only acting, but a certain amount of privilege comes with the status. I can make the rules mine. I can change anything and everything to suit the new club I wish to create. Thing is, I want the club to be better—not just be a new dictator at the helm. Yeah, the Bows have been the bad guys, and we need that fixed. That's in my mind first and foremost. But she'll be beside me as I take down King and create the Broken Bows that should've been long ago.

Watching her bent over to start the water, I find myself thinking what it would be like to sink myself into her ass. Gripping her thick hips, holding her as she screams my name. That would be pure perfection.

Placing my hands on her bare ass, I massage and grip the globes tightly. Dipping a finger within her cheeks, I rub against her entrance.

"I want to be here," I growl. She probably won't agree, but I have a driving need to touch her everywhere. Moving my fingers between her sweet cunt from behind, I drag the lubrication along her ass.

It feels nice, I won't deny that.

"Who said anyone has, and that you have the right to it?" Her tone is sultry.

Pushing against the barrier, I swirl my finger gently against it. Her body stills, then relaxes at my touch. But still, she doesn't outright say yes or no. I won't force her.

Reaching back, she moves my hands off her ass. "I need a shower, but I can easily go to the spare bathroom I found down the hall if I need to."

Laughing deeply, I switch tactics. Reaching around to her nipples, I pinch each of them as my cock buries itself between her warm cheeks. "I'll leave you today, Obi, but we'll have that conversation again." Rubbing myself along her body, she's trying my resolve and my control as she pushes her hips back to meet my strokes.

Obi rises to her full height. Not much of a change really from bent over, but she steps within the shower, leaving me and my hard-on alone.

"On second thought, you can use the other bathroom, sir." Closing the door with a smirk, using it as a barrier between us, she laughs. I laugh in turn.

Since I left my family, I can count on one hand how many times I've laughed. True joy has been missing in my life. Death, destruction, and duty. None of those have happiness associated.

Honor and trust don't ask for humor, or for my joy. Obi doesn't ask for it, and I guess that's why it's easier to be happy around her.

I'm not about to let her rule me either. I slide the door back. "I'm not using a different bathroom in my own home, woman. Shift over, I—"

With a loud ding, the doorbell rings out.

Who the fuck would drop by here?

All I know is that it better not be King. I'll kill a DEA agent today if it is.

Don't mess with a man and his ass.

"This isn't over, woman. I'll be right back." Closing the glass door, I leave the bathroom with a heavy thunk of the door. Putting on my discarded jeans, I know it's him.

It has to be. No one else would show up here, and he'll pay for his arrogance.

Chapter

O ubliette

     Standing in the shower, alone, I gave myself an ultimatum: I won't give in like a whore. I'm not one and I won't be one. If he wants something from me, he'll work for it. By the time I've dried off and dressed, he hasn't returned, which has me wondering what's going on?

Wandering down the hall toward the living room, I hear Lucius, and he sounds pissed.

"I asked for your help for *her*. It was a one-time thing, King."

"And it opened up our relationship again, brother." The other man's voice is dark and condescending, sounding smug and satisfied with himself.

"I'm not your *brother*. I was your way in. I was the punk kid you blamed a whole fucking club's problems on."

"I was never satisfied with one club, Lucius. The Intentions were the in I needed to start my career. You knew that. And now, you're giving me more. You may not like it, but you don't have a choice."

Stepping around the corner, the man with the voice looks my way. His smile is distasteful.

"She'll give it to me if you won't. Won't you, sweet, sweet Oubliette?" He sneers at me. Who the fuck is this guy? How does he know me?

He's the same size as Lucius, and nearly as deadly looking, in a weird sort of way. His style is perfectly polished. His cornrows are pulled back into a low ponytail. His bright, light brown eyes search me from head to foot, giving me the heebie-jeebies.

With a dress shirt that's pressed and rolled at the sleeves, showcasing his multitude of tattoos, the perfectly tapered casual pants and loafers—not to forget the gun attached at his hip, he's well-appointed and deadly.

"Leave her the fuck out of this, King. She has nothing to do with any of it." Stomping across the room, out for blood, Lucius looks ready to kill.

I see the insanity taking form. It's like watching a car wreck, or a final moment before the hero falls off the train and dies. The end is tragic to watch.

Leaping across the room, with a fist into the side of the guy's head, Lucius connects with a crack. Blood spatters around the kitchen as an all-out war ensues. Left-right, left-right, the two of them trade hits. I step back into the hallway, away from them, as they cause each other maximum damage.

Spitting blood, King laughs as he stands, ready to strike again. Lucius doesn't wait. Turning and laying shot after shot to King's midsection and head, it's wearing him down. It's wearing them both down. As King falters, and when it seems that the two are almost done, Lucius lunges with a left to King's right knee. Buckling, King falls to his knees with a grunt.

"Stay down, asshole." Pointing at him, Lucius pulls out a bar chair, huffing, and takes a seat. "She's not in this. Never again will she be used. You hear me, Mr. DEA? Never. And while we're on the topic, keep your hands out of my club."

"Your club?" Rising slowly off the floor, babying that knee, King stands and wipes his face on that once pristine shirt. "Fine, Mr. President. I'll leave her out, but you've gotta bring me what I want." He spits on the floor. "Remember, I always get what I want. Unless you want to renegotiate your previous—"

Rising fast, with a strength I didn't think he'd have left in him, Lucius links his hand at King's neck. Holding him to the wall, I see his jaw tick. The muscles strain as he holds his anger at bay and King aloft. "My family is clear of your sights. She's not in your sights. And my club? My club has protection. You follow?"

"It'll cost ya." Even as everything is out of his favor, this King guy shows balls. I'm equally thrilled and frightened by that. What wouldn't he do if given the chance? Men like him are scary when cornered.

"No. You don't get it, Magnus. It'll cost *you*. I've paid my debt." Releasing him from the wall, Lucius steps back. "Now get the fuck out of my house and out of my face. Then return Scarlet. No questions asked, no further issues with the club. We do what we do and you wait."

With a slight limp, King moves toward the door. "I'll get what I want. You'll *bring* me what I want." Licking his lips, he smiles my way. "Scarlet can be a keen friend if you can't find us what we want, Lucius."

"She's released in an hour, King. No movement on that."

With a wave, he states over his shoulder, "I'll be in touch."

Once the door shuts and King has finally left, Lucius stands up the tossed over stool. Taking a heavy seat, leaning on the counter, he reaches out for a towel that rests close by.

Moving from the hallway and into the kitchen, I stand quietly.

"Fuck me." His tone is calmer now, but I'm still wary of coming within range.

His temper is scary.

He was intense.

"Do you mind getting me some ice, Obi?"

"Ah, sure." Grabbing a cupful, Lucius opens the tea towel for me to drop it in.

Watching as he scrunches it up and places it at his temple, with a small smile he says, "Thanks." Looking around the room, taking in the damage and mess, his tone is gentle once more. "Why does that man have to invade my life over and over again?"

I'm unsure if he means that to be rhetorical or if he's waiting for an answer, so I stay quiet. Being around the Army for so long, I've learned the art of keeping quiet when necessary. Speaking up garners trouble.

"Mind giving me my phone, love?"

Handing it to him, Lucius hits one button while adjusting the ice to the other side. I don't hear the phone connect, but he starts speaking. "Munch. Church in an hour." The other person answers quickly before Lucius continues. "Yeah, check on him...No...Yeah, she's worked out...Got it." Without a goodbye, he hangs up and lays the phone on the counter.

I didn't think it could be possible, but he looks more stressed out. Waiting for him to speak, I start to tidy the counter.

"I'll bet you're wondering what that was about."

It's a statement, not a question. Again, I don't speak.

Releasing the makeshift ice pack from his face, Lucius looks my way. "I've always been in the club life—born into it, but not this club."

Standing up, he grips the whiskey bottle we'd been drinking from. Uncorking it, Lucius takes a few deep gulps. Wiping his mouth on the towel and dumping the ice in the sink, he continues. "My parents were a part of the Cruel Intentions MC out of New York. My dad was the president. Even though their club ran human trafficking over the Canadian border, they weren't bad people. They thought we'd been kept out of it as kids, but we weren't oblivious. We knew. They were good at it too, until King and his *agents* showed up. They jacked the whole club, sending pretty much every member, old lady, and family that was old enough to jail or juvie.

"At the time, he offered me an option: I could learn to be an agent and help take down clubs from the inside. I'd be his little pet project. It was that or watch my family be destroyed. He'd threatened to toss my little brother Cody in jail as an adult, my sister Dejene would be sent to children's aid, and I'd have the label of snitch. I was about to turn seventeen, so it left me with little or no choice. I did what I had to."

Pacing the room, I wait as Lucius continues. "I knew I had to do it. King trained me, kept me in his clutches, then when he knew I had no other choice, he set me loose in Nor Cal with the only thing I knew better than myself—a bike. I ran for years on autopilot, riding and hopping from place to place. I didn't have a club or a home. I slept under the stars and lived on the beach. That's when I met True. He had this weird obsession with the sunrise. He loved to see it on the day after a full moon. He appreciated my ride and we got to talking.

"No matter how I broke it down, I only knew club life. It was my home. Joining the Bows was as natural as breathing. I patched in fast, jumped the ranks fast, and never heard from King. I thought he was done with me. I thought I was clear of his shit, but I wasn't. Out on a run a few months back, our cargo was hit. DEA. They were there waiting for us. I wrote it off, but then a week later we were ambushed again. The more I looked into it, King was at the bottom of it all.

Taking another large gulp from the bottle, he sets it to the counter. "One day, I was left a note that only I would understand. A playing card—the fucking King of Spades with a phone number on it—stuck to the handle of my ride." Turning my way, he looks me deep in the eyes. "That was the number I called to get you free. I called King, knowing that saving you was going to cause me to fall back into his clutches."

Me? "Why? Why would you? If you were out, why not stay out? I meant nothing to you."

"But that's where you're wrong." Stepping around the counter, he stands over me. "The day I met with Death, I saw this tiny bartender at Humble. Strong, defiant, and sexy as fuck. Then, seeing you walking out of that limo, fearful and yet still defiant at the warehouse, I had hopes that True was fucking joking. Thing was, you were pushed further than anyone I know, and you kept coming back stronger than I thought you could be. Even with Nock and his sick antics, you made sure you had the upper hand. I saw a certain pride in your defiant nature. I wanted more." Playing with my wet braid again, toying with the ends, he smiles. A huge smile that makes even his upper lip rise. "This compact little woman was showing up a hardened biker. He should have broken you, but you won. I knew I needed to save you. I knew you couldn't stay there." He pulls me tight to his chest. "Obi, I'm not giving you up to the likes of King. I'm not giving you up at all."

Well, shit. That's one of the nicest things he's said.

Bending low, pressing his lips to mine, the tang of his blood is sharp, but his soft lips are scrumptious. Running a hand down his abs, there's a sharp intake of breath.

Breaking the kiss, I smile sneakily. "How about that shower? I'll tend to your boo-boos."

With a quirk of his head, and a *'you've gotta be kidding me'* glare, Lucius nods. "Bring it on, little lady."

Chapter

Busta

Oubliette took that way better than I thought she would. I basically told her that I'm a NARK, a pitiful man that has been lying to his friends and his brothers. Someone who's working with the DEA. A stupid motherfucker that broke the trust of his brothers, all because of her. Even seeing King and I toe-to-toe in my living room, she didn't run down the hall and out the front door, vowing to call the cops.

Like it would do any good. King would just make it all go away.

So, now what?

Well, now I have to come due on the deal I brokered with Death. I have to run a club and fucking fix it. Plus, I have to come clean on the deal with King too. Within all of that, I have to somehow find a way to keep my ass out of the grave. Jail isn't an option, I'd just get shanked as soon as my trainers hit the gen-pop floor.

So now I have to get creative.

First things first. I need a shower, another round of sex with this woman, and a plan.

Leading her down the hall to the bathroom, Oubliette silently walks beside me. I can see the wheels turning as she moves, considering everything I've told her, but she's entertained and intrigued as to where we might go. I see it.

Stripping off my blood spotted jeans, lifting her now blood smattered white tee, we stand in the shower once more. The water stings against the cuts, but they fuel the rage that simmers inside. The wheels of cunning shit will start after this. But for now, the wheels of cunnilingus will turn instead.

"Stand there and don't move," I growl out as the water trickles down her form.

"Don't fucking move, Obi," I say as she's about to move. Smacking her hard on the ass, Oubliette grins wide. Taking a seat on the built-in bench, I motion her toward me with a finger waggle. Stepping slowly—too slow for my tastes—I pull her by the ass cheeks toward me. Sinking my mouth between those soft folds again, I stroke her softness.

"Holy fuck! Lucius, I—" Squealing, her arms shoot out to hold her upright against the wall and sliding glass door. That gives me an idea. Licking her until her body is wobbly and her release is close, I reposition her against the glass doors.

"Stay there." Stepping close, rubbing my erection against her backside, I allow it to dip between her cheeks, pushing her legs out slightly. I don't have a condom, but I can't resist the opportunity to sink between her hot heat once more. "I want you, Oubliette. I want to fill you up until you scream my name."

I rub her ass against me. "So what the fuck are you waiting for, Busta?" Cheeky woman.

"I need to go grab a condom."

"In for a penny, mister. In for a penny." She pulls me close to her, and thrusting within, filling her and feeling her body squeeze me for more, I move to the sounds of her breathless sighs. Each time I push forward, I watch her face. Turned sideways against the glass, her grin grows and her eyes close. "More, please. I'm so close."

I give her everything—every move I have in my arsenal in this position. I grind, pull out to the tip, and slowly rise within her, slamming hard, quick, and with a precision that seems to make her fall apart.

We do that until the water runs cool.

On a sigh, she releases, and I do too shortly after her. No pomp and circumstance, just unbridled lust. Washing up fast, toweling and heading back to my bed with the sun dipping low, we're sated.

It took me a bit, but as my mind reeled through all the scenarios, considering everything I wish to do to King, I'm amazed I'm this calm.

Thinking of everything he deserves for all he's done. Scrolling through my mental rolodex, everyone I can involve that will assist in his demise. I catalogue new uses for tools that I'd never considered.

He'll pay.

As Oubliette is softly snoring beside me, I remind myself of the game plan. Without the intention of it, the two of us fall asleep entwined.

Chapter

O**ubliette**
     Coming to his clubhouse wasn't something I expected to do. Like, ever. But Lucius told me he had a meet at the club, and that we should've been there hours ago. We'd fallen asleep. Waking with a start when he'd caught himself with drool, we were out the door in minutes. Stopping on the street around the corner from the clubhouse, Lucius shut down the bike and hopped off.

"Obi, have you been in a clubhouse before?"

"Yeah, with Jasmine."

"I'll be tied up in a meeting for a bit, but I'll leave you with the old ladies. They'll take care of you. You'll be safe." Pacing in front of his semi-heated bike, Lucius is rattled. He says I'll be safe, but in some way, he seems kind of unnerved.

I don't know this man well enough to really chat him up or make jokes to loosen the mood, so once more, I stay quiet and wait. Moving back and forth, thinking through things, the traffic blasts by us. They're oblivious to his internal war.

"Obi. The Broken Bows in the past haven't been the good guys. I'm going to change that. I need time to. But when you go there, remember they're still expecting the same—a status quo. Don't be shocked. And most of all, do me a favor and don't run. I won't have time to chase you down while I'm in church."

Considering everything that I've gone through, all the things that have changed between Lucius and I, I nod. "I can go on a little faith."

Smoothing out his beard, he smiles weakly. "Thank you, Obi."

"Explain to me what you can later though, okay?"

"Got it, lady. And Obi?" Stepping back across the seat, he starts up his bike. "I've never brought a woman to the club, so it could make you a bit of a sideshow."

Wrapping my hands around his waist, stroking the front of his jeans, I smile into his Broken Bows rocker. "No problem."

Laughing, he pulls away from the curb. "While you're there, I'm Busta."

· · · ·

PULLING UP TO THE CLUBHOUSE, parking the bike and starting for the doors, Lucius smacks my ass. Wandering in and bringing me in behind him, Lucius—I mean, Busta, leads the way.

Entering, taking in the dark, dank, and seedy feeling space, I let my eyes adjust. To the left there are women and men in varying acts of attraction. There are guys playing pool at a worn-out table, a few just chillin' in chairs or chatting on phones. There's also a good-looking older guy behind a fully stocked bar. The bar is the cleanest and most modern part of the room as far as I can see, which makes me wary of touching anything.

As Busta travels the space—with every eye on us—he stops at the foot of a tiny elderly woman with short hair, a bright smile, and the typical clubhouse look. It suits her. The majority of the group with their tiny shirts, or non-existent shirts, short shorts and oversized earring hoops, look like hookers straight off the corner. I don't know much about the Bows, as Lucius calls them, but to me, there's a decidedly large difference between the Bows and the Army.

In the Hade's Army, the hierarchy ranges, and the clubhouse is airy, clean, and decidedly bright. Here it's dark, dangerous, and dirty feeling. Also, I'm out of place, and the staring speaks louder than words. The Broken Bows are an African American club, which means every face in the crowd is eyeing me up. Blonde, blue eyed, petite in stature. I'm an anomaly.

Sure, the boys from Hade's Army have that 'you look out of place' too, but Death, his sister Jazzy, and his little brother treat me like family. Their club is multinational—Native American, Korean, African

American, and my favorite guitarist, Destroyer, won't say more than that he's Canadian. I feel like I fit into their quirky puzzle.

From across the room, I realize I've paused in my steps when Lucius calls my name. "Oubliette, come here."

Walking over, standing beside him, he smiles down at me as he places a hand on the shoulder of the lady with the short hair. "This is Pan."

She grins wide up at Busta. "Hi, Oubliette. I'm Pandora. Busta here calls me Panna, or Pan for short." Holding out a hand she offers, I shake it in return.

"You'll be fine here with Panna." Kissing me lightly on the head, he starts away. "I'll be about an hour or so, but you'll be fine."

"You said that twice." Winking, I smile at him. "I'll be just fine, Lu—Busta," I correct myself before I call him Lucius.

The look on Pandora's face says it all. He's not called Lucius *here*. He said to call him Busta, so from now on, that's what I'll call him.

Feeling he's left me in capable hands, he turns his sights on the guys in the room and yells out, "Church. Now."

Stomping away down a hall, he's gone. As are a large deal of the men. Some kiss their girls, others do up their jeans or wipe their mouths, but all saunter away behind Lucius.

Chapter

O<u>ubliette</u>
Standing in the now emptied room, feeling like one of those colorful fish in a tiny bag, the room is decidedly different. The men have left Pandora and a few other ladies, younger guys without patches on their cuts, and the man behind the bar.

Pandora taps me on the shoulder and smiles, knocking me out of the inspection. "Come, sit. You look a little bewildered."

Exactly. "Overwhelmed is more like it. It's been a whirlwind."

With a laugh that sounds like tinkling chimes, Pandora smiles. "Come on. Come have a drink and tell me about you then. We'll start with the easy stuff, and work up to the hard junk."

I shake my head. "I'm good. I don't need a—"

"Of course you do. You've been through a ton and I'm sure we have your brew. Right, Quiver?"

"Anything for you, Panna, and your new friend here." Setting down the cup with others, his sweet smile lights up the room. "I'm Monty. Everyone calls me Quiver, though."

"Oubliette," I say, taking a seat.

"What's your poison, little lady?"

After the days that have led up to this, I go for the gusto. "Tequila. Two shots, no lime, but I'd be happy with a bottle of sriracha."

Scowling, he shows me his distaste. "That sounds awful, but what the lady wants..."

"Then make it three and give it a try. You'll find it's not bad at all." Pouring the shots, I inspect Quiver. He's around my height, five-five or so. Stout, over thirty I'd say, judging by the few grays. Strong arms with tattoos that course each. Dark eyes, light skin, and a sweet smile. "No way, girl. I can't do that. My ulcer would explode." He taps his slightly rotund stomach. "That's why I'm the bartender. It keeps the profits in the business."

"Makes sense." Swiping up the sriracha, dribbling a few drops in each shot, I pick up the first one and down it quick. The fire and flare rushes straight to my blood. It feels perfect.

Better than coffee.

Grabbing the second, I down it just as quick in the same manner and lick my lips. "Line up two more, please."

"Thought you didn't wanna drink?" Quiver man-giggles as he pours.

"Guess I changed my mind based on the lovely companions."

Looking at Pandora, her wide eyes tell me more than words could. "Run it down. I'm a pretty good listener."

"Not much to tell. I'm a bartender at a club and I have a big brother." Pandora's company and sweet smile makes me feel at ease. I don't know if saying I work at a rival club, that I was kidnapped, and subsequently I've been having sex with Lucius is really any of her business, so I keep that to myself.

"Here, Pan." Placing a white wine before her, Quiver goes back to polishing glasses.

"Thanks, Quiv." Picking it up, she turns to me. "That seemed like the edited CliffsNotes version, but for now, I'll take it. You don't know me and I don't know you. But if you feel like you need someone, I'm here. I've been around long enough with Retribution, my partner, that I know where the bodies are buried, as it were."

I wouldn't doubt that. To be honest, she probably helped over the years to bury them.

Sucking back on one of the newly setup shots, I smile. "True enough."

"Look, Oubliette, it's not my business, but I'm gonna give you a bit of insight. In the five or so years that young man has been here, I've yet to see him wander in with a girl—woman or otherwise. He toys with the whores but that's it. He's never been solid on anyone. And I can say he's never sweet enough to lay a kiss on a forehead and worry that they're in the right hands." With a wink, she picks up her glass and starts away. "I'll be over there waiting on Ret. If you feel like joining, I promise the ladies will be good to you. If you'd rather sit here with Quiver, that's fine too. Just do Busta a favor. Don't walk off."

"Thanks. I'll consider that." With a nod, she walks off to the far side of the room, leaving me and Quiver at the bar.

Staying put, only because the bar feels appropriate to me, we talk about stupid drink shit for a while. It leads, of course, to further shots, dumb conversations about movies, politics, and the true reason women buy lingerie, but I enjoy the time as it passes.

Setting my latest soldier on the counter, I rise. "Which way to the bathroom, Quiver?"

"Down there, third door on the right."

"Thanks," I say as I wander on wobbly legs down the hall farthest from the meeting, and away from the common area. Counting down until I hit the third door, I push it open, nearly knocking over a woman that I thought was leaving. She bounces the door closed behind me.

"Hi," I say with a drunk grin. "'Scuse me."

"You don't belong here."

"Don't I know that," I mutter.

"Then why are you here?" she asks, all attitude.

"Busta brought me here for safe keeping."

"Well, you can just walk your pristine little ass right out the front and keep on walkin'." Laying a hand on the door to the stall, she blocks my way. I really, really need to pee. Her stopping me is probably not the best idea. My fight or flight always ramps up with bitches that think they know what's best for me.

Placing a hand on the same door, right beside hers, I smile sweetly. "Cunt much? Get out of my way. I need to pee, and I don't have time for your pissing match. Get it? *Pissing* match?" My addled brain thinks it's worth the humor, but I'm pretty sure it's going to lead to a catfight.

"This isn't a music festival in the valley." Not the first time I've been picked on for my hobo chic attire and windswept hair, but I'm wearing Busta's T-shirt and my short shorts. Right now, it's more boyfriend hobo. "You think you belong here? That you can come here and cause trouble? Busta doesn't want you. You're a toy. A trophy. The white chick he can bang and say he's had one. Just remember, he'll always return to a sister. We can give him what he wants."

Laughing out loud at her audacity and blatant stupidity, I see her seething inside. "Bitch, get out of my way. If you want to fight me after I pee, game on. But I doubt you want me peeing on your Walmart specials." Pushing on the door, causing her to release it, I step in and lock it. Releasing the building pressure in my bladder as fast as I can, I hear her outside the door, tapping her dime-store hooker shoes on the floor. I've dealt with whores and strippers at Humble for years, and this one is no different. Every woman wants to mark their territory on the man they think is theirs. She's just doing it right off the bat with the wrong girl. I'll give her points for the lady balls she owns, though. She doesn't know anything of me, and it's funny she already assumes I'm a threat.

No worries, sweetheart. I am.

Popping the lock, stepping out and proceeding to wash my hands, the girl stands to the side with her arms crossed and a sly look on her face. Drying my hands, I turn her way. "So?"

Taking a step forward, uncurling her arms and stretching out to hit me, I duck. That was so televised it wasn't funny. Swinging again, I duck again.

"If you're going to hit me, get on with it," I taunt her. Not my best idea, but she's sluggish, and a really poor fighter.

Taking another swing, I smack it away. Being a bit cocky, I don't notice the wild open-handed smack coming on the right. I feel the sting where her ring hits me, and I realize she'd turned it around.

Striking out wildly, with no rhyme or reason to her throws, she continues, hoping to connect. Luckily, I swing out and connect with her jaw. Shocked, she takes a step back, cradling her face as if I'd broken her teeth.

"You hit me! I did nothing to you! Busta will hear about this!" Tears start, total alligator tears, but tears nonetheless as she starts for the door.

Pulling it open and running down the hall, she screams and carries on. What a fake cunt.

Shit.

She set me up for that.

Looking at the cut along my cheek just below my eye, I cuss. Dabbing it with water and a moist cloth, I try to cool the marred skin. Now I have a mark on me, and that will be a conversation with Busta I'm not looking forward to.

Shit.

I would feel welcomed by the women, he said.

I'd feel at home, he said.

Bullshit.

I call bullshit, Lucius.

Chapter

B<u>usta</u>

"Run it down," I say once the door closes.

The first order of business—picking a new president. By default, when True died, I took the reins. Thing is, I wanted a change in the club, which then made that position precarious. To take the seat by force, to take it by default, or to define the position by what the old guard had, that wouldn't change anything. I needed the votes cast. It had to be from the members directly.

This shit was about to go diplomatic. Like other clubs. Like my family's club.

Like the Army.

Munch, the man who loves numbers almost as much as he loves Gazelle, reads off the vote. "With thirty-eight votes total, from the main and satellite clubs, there were twenty-seven for Busta and eleven for Blaze." Looking my way, he lays out the votes. I know what it means.

"Busta is the new president by vote."

To say I'm shocked is an understatement. I'm fucking floored. I thought for sure the boys would vote more for Blaze—a man who was born into this club—and less for me. Though it seems a few of those brothers voted my way.

I'll do my fucking damnedest to honor those votes and show them I can do good things with this club.

"Okay." Taking the empty seat at the end of the table and moving the gavel to the side, I take up the mantle of president. "Let's get down to it then." Running out the ideas I've had on how to team up with the other clubs in the area, and how to run a cleaner club, I tell them how it is in my mind. We'll vote this shit out until we have a solid agreement on our hands as a family and as a stronger club. It could take a few meets, but I'm not about to give King and his goons further reasons to run us up to Chino or San Q. We're going legit.

After a couple hours behind the closed doors, we're just as indecisive in our changes as we were when we walked in. Now I understand why DG was a dictator. With shouting, cursing, threats—some idle and others downright deadly, I'm losing my patience. Thank fuck we don't allow weapons in here. I'd have shot at least six of my brothers for their childish bickering.

We've been stuck on the business of the cartel and our supply run of flesh. The cursing, whining, and pouting about a loss in profits has left us sounding like a bitchy bunch of cocksuckers.

Rubbing my temples and cracking my neck to release the tension, I'm reminded that I left Obi out there in the care of women she doesn't know. Yeah, Obi has handled everything in stride, but it's still a lot to ask of her to deal with.

"You fuckin' kidding me! They won't be happy losing profits. The Alta Noche won't like us exiting the business. They'd make us pay for it." Flight is right, but he's not giving me a solution. None of them are.

"Who gives a shit about Alta? They're not *our* club. If our pres wants to go legit, to find other sources of income, then why aren't we figuring this out instead of bitching like whores?" Munch pipes up. His natural, subtle calm is stewing.

I've watched him. For the past hour, he's doodled on his notepad, laying out numbers, thoughts, and stacks of scribblings from his analytical brain.

"Whatcha got then, Munch?" I ask, knowing he has something devised, and I, myself, would like to know what it is.

Yeah, I know he wants out of here to check on Gazelle. After the knife incident, she's been in his charge twenty-four seven. She stays in his quarters, bedridden, and under strict orders to be careful. He still won't admit he loves her, or at the least that he cares for her. I now understand why he's antsy to check on her. I am with Obi too.

Leaning over his notepad, tapping it with his pen, I watch as he worries the inside of his cheek.

"Well, I see it this way. You want legit, right? We don't need further heat because we leave the Alta, and I think we've had enough of all-out war with the Army and Bastards." Looking to me, I nod in agreement. "You have an understanding with Death, right?"

"Yeah, I think we're on terms that suit us both. Why?" I ask.

He looks at Miss. "You still have a sister at the Bastards?"

"Yeah. Josie's with the VP, Sinner. What are ya thinking, bro?" Josie and Single Miss are twins. Both dark, tall, lanky, and scary as fuck. Each are kind of fucked in their own way, and simply twisted. I guess that's why I made sure to sway the votes to make him the replacement for me. He's the new enforcer, a perfect position for him. I know he'll do what's needed when the club needs it.

"Can you give her a shout and see if we can arrange a sit?" Munch still hasn't explained his plan, but I know his idea of tying up the space between the clubs could be a good thing. Especially when we're dealing with King. Only Death and I have an understanding, and it's time we brought the Heartless Bastards in on it.

Turning his pad toward us, Munch squints. "This is going to be a monster coup to pull off, but when we're done, I think we'll come out on top."

Plowing through it, flipping pages, showing us the numbers, the facts of his mastermind fuckery, I feel a sudden sense of gaiety. We're going to do this. We're going to do this as a club, moving forward from the past.

We'll be stronger for it.

When he's all done, Munch has the full agreement of the room.

Finally, something we can agree on—money.

Relaxing back in my chair, I lift the gavel off the table. "We done for today, brothers?" With a resounding silence, most nod their agreement. "Good, because my ass is fucking numb from sitting here."

Hitting the gavel on the block for the first time, the vibration courses through my hand in a wonderful way. I'm creating the club we should've had all along, the kind I should've had all along in the Cruel Intentions back home.

While brothers rise and leave, others step over and pat me on the back or shake my hand. I appreciate it all. It's still surreal, though. Looking down at my cut, the one that needs adjustments in patches, I still don't believe I'm the head of this helm.

"Good to see you," Blaze states as he approaches me with a firm handshake and a smile. "The right man will be the one who fixes us. I know you'll lead us right."

"I'll do what's right. I won't lead like DG." I won't speak ill of the dead, but a heavy-handed leadership didn't do the club right. We were more a gang of thugs than a biker club. "I knew we needed a change, and I think this will be the right way. We couldn't keep losing membership to a bullet."

"Exactly. And I'm glad you have a—" Pausing, Blaze looks to the hallway. "What the fuck you think's going on out there?"

Hearing loud shouting, it causes us to halt and listen.

Fuck. Obi.

"Hey, mind if we chat more later? I have to check on a guest."

He grins wide, showcasing his bright white teeth. "Yeah, go."

Stepping out into the hall, the shouting and cursing grows louder. I don't hear Oubliette exactly, but I'm not sure if that leaves me more or less fearful.

Walking into the common area, the guys are settled around the bar, along with the majority of the women. Even Panna. I don't remember her letting her 'weave down' before, but there she is with shots lined up, sucking back one after the other, facing the bartender and racing to the end of the small cups. Quiver hasn't drank in years—his ulcer taking its toll—so I know it's not him. Thing is, I don't see *who* it is.

I have a feeling, though.

"Cocksucker! Cocksucker!" A few of the brothers recite, laughing and grinning.

Approaching the bar, I look down the line. I knew it. "Fine, I'll make more." Waving her hands in a downward motion, swinging them as if she's calming, and not causing a clamor, Obi looks right at home. I forgot how fucking sexy she looked behind the bar mixing drinks at Humble, and I'm floored to watch her now. It's perfection. Pouring them into the shooters, lighting them up with matches and throwing her personal sparkle to them, Obi slips one across to Pan.

Picking it up and downing it quick, she blows out a hot breath of smoke. "You're supposed to hold it in. Swallow, woman!" Obi yells, laughing before she sees me down the counter.

"Busta!" She grins before her face falls. "Or should I say, President Busta?"

I step in front of her. "How long have you been the bartender?"

Shrugging with half-closed lids, she pinches two fingers together. "For a bit."

Looking at her straight on, I see the shiner that's taking shape.

"Who the fuck hit you, Obi?"

The room stills, the jubilation dying down, and the brothers start to slowly shift away from the bar with their girls in tow. "I'm fine, Busta. It's a scratch."

"Obi," I say, grinding my teeth together. My nerves that were once relaxed are now ramping back up to cause havoc.

"Busta."

"I'm trying to be calm." Cracking my knuckles and teasing the end of my beard—my nervous twitch when I'm bothered—I try to stay relaxed. "Oubliette, how did you gain that mark?"

"Do you want a shooter? Something fiery and fun? Or are you into a sweet chocolate concoction?" Ignoring my request and turning her back to me, she grabs up a few liquor bottles from the bar. "I'll go for the sweet one. You look like you could use it."

Blowing out a heavy breath, starting toward the back of the bar, everyone in the way parts like the sea, or ventures off to other parts of the clubhouse, away from my intended course. Lifting the arm and stepping inside, I park my body in her way. "Now Busta, how am I supposed to make you a great drink if you're in the way?"

It's easy to see that she's fully fucking drunk. I also notice the cut isn't as small as I thought. The bruising around the edges of it are already turning blue and purple, and it suits the shape of a knuckle. Gripping her by the hips, propping her ass on the bar, I feather a hand across her face. Wincing slightly, she turns away quickly, then turns back with a big grin.

"It's not bad, Lucius," she whispers.

"Obi, who hit you? I don't take it lightly. I can see it hurts. I won't leave it until you tell me," I implore her as calmly as I can.

Touching my face, she runs her fingers through my beard. "It was a girly spat. Nothin' you need to worry about." I look over at Panna, one of the only people who stayed put at the bar. Obi implores her with her own look, a look that says 'help me.'

Without turning to her, I ask, "Pandora, what happened to my girl here?"

"Your girl?" Obi recites with a snappy look.

I place a finger on Oubliette's lips. "Shush. I'm talking to Pandora." She grins, and I feel her tight giggle that attempts to escape.

"She had a run—"

"Pan! You promised. New girl and new rules!" Oubliette yells out, laughing the whole time. It's good to see she's getting along with someone that I trust and care for. Pan is my favorite woman here. She's more like a mother than just a member of the club to me.

"Pres, there was a scuffle in the bathroom. Don't worry, though, your *girl* here got in a few good licks to Mona."

Fucking Mona. I thought she was dealt with.

"You said you'd keep quiet, Pan." Oubliette pouts.

"I said I'd keep quiet unless he asked. He asked."

With a resounding, *Pandora!* yelled across the room, she rises from the bar and starts away. "Ret's calling. Good luck, Oubliette. See you around."

"See ya," Oubliette calls out, but her look shows the disappointment of being outed and left alone to deal with the aftermath.

"Obi, I'm tired, I'm stressed, and I have a ton on my mind. Tell me what happened."

With downturned eyes, and a puffed-out bottom lip, she says, "Don't make me tell you. I didn't expect any less. I held my own, we worked it out and I'm fine. Leave it, please, Lucius."

Knowing eyes are on us from all directions, I let it rest. "We'll talk about this later."

With a wink and a grin, Obi pushes me to back away. Hopping down on wobbly legs, she smacks her hands together. "Right. Time for a drink. Celebrations I hear, President."

Oubliette

Oh, for fuck. I shouldn't have had that last Widowmaker. Or the last two Cocksuckers.

Probably should've avoided the Inky Mermaid Piss, and the Sinful Heartbreaker too, because I'm pretty sure the Talented Mr. Rip-my-ass-a-new-one is ready to kill me. At least that's the impression I get from his gaze.

I'm intoxicated. There's no doubting that, but I think I deserve to let my hair down after all the shit I've gone through lately.

Sucking on my fingers, clearing the vermouth that dribbled as I mixed the last set of shooters, I look across at the lineup of boys at the bar. Yeah, a bunch have ran off to hang with their women, but a great deal of them were interested in what I could create.

"Oubliette, these drinks are spectacular," Flight calls out, slurring his words.

Lining up a few shooters, I concentrate on pouring into the small mouthed cups. "I'm a fucking genius for drinks. I should write a book."

"You got that right." Miss slaps a hand on the bar. The motion throws him off-balance, tossing his ass to the floor as he rocks off the chair.

"Fuck, brother. You're cut off," Flight jokes, laughing and reaching for his own shooter. We've been at this for a few hours now, and Flight is someone I'm starting to enjoy the company of. His short hair, tight to his head in tiny waves—with cutouts in the back, creating a pattern of flights on an arrow, he's meticulous and good-looking. Not to miss that sweet smile, I see why the ladies flock to his side as we drink. Though, most of those *ladies* are lightweights, and they've ran off for other entertainment.

As a few of the guys gather up Miss, who's told me to call him Parker, I laugh. Well, I laughed until I looked at the stoic and solemn face across from me.

Lucius.

He's kept his wits about him. He's nursed beers instead of delving into the *'world of Oubliette and her wicked liquids'*—his words, not mine.

"I'm done for tonight," Miss states. His stance sways as he tries to gain his footing. "These earthquakes are killing me. When will the ground stop moving?"

Laughing out, Flight smacks him on the shoulder as he grips him around the waist to hold him up. "There's no earthquake, you quack. It's you that's movin.'"

Allowing his brothers to hold him up, Miss grins wide. "Probably true. I should go."

He's talked more and more as the liquid's loosened his tongue. The man is fucked. He is well and fucked. When I tried to give him *bartender advice,* Lucius gave me the 'don't do it' look. I've stayed quiet and only listened.

Removing the hands of his brothers, that are the only things keeping him upright, he tumbles to the floor once more. Miss is a towering hulk of a man. He's easily the same, if not more than Lucius is in weight. They're just shy of each other in height, and his body exudes a dangerous aura. The scars that course his neck and arms tell me he's taken and dealt it back in spades to his enemies. It has to be the reason he's been promoted to enforcer. I'd be fucking scared of his ass if he came looking for me.

After years in the club life—well, at least surrounded by it at work—I've come to sort out the dangerous from the showy. I can tell you who's in control of their tendencies to cause death versus the guy who falls into it because he had to. Lucius learned to be the bad guy.

Miss? He's fought his way out of the darkness to be the weapon he is now. He's honed it to perfection.

"Time to go, Oubliette." Standing up and laying his empty beer bottle on the counter, Lucius motions for me to end our night.

I get it, and in a way, I can't disagree. I'm fucking beat. The fight with the club girl Mona didn't do anything other than use up some of my reserve adrenaline, and now that I've burnt away the rest of my strength with booze and laughter, I'm bushed.

Smacking my hands together, I swipe them back and forth, like they do when you're at the casinos. "Time for me to go, boys. Thanks for the night."

"Really?" A few call out, but I've made my decision. Well, actually, Busta did, but I'm following suit.

"Yeah. My ride's heading out. At this point, I should be sober enough that I can grip his hips to hold on. If I keep drinking I'll be roadkill."

A few of the guys approach me and thank me, and a few tell Busta how I have to come back for a club night to bartend. Miss and Flight let their Pres know that if he doesn't name me as property, that he'll have competition.

I'm not sure I want that—the property title—but I know the benefits of it, so it doesn't bother me to be called that.

Stepping in to the outstretched arm of Lucius, I curl into his side. Kissing me on the forehead, he leads us outside to his bike. As I hit the pavement, it shifts uncomfortably. "I might've had a few too many," I groan, swaying slightly in the lamplight.

"Well, if you hold here," he advises, placing my hand on his cock, "it should be enough of a handle to keep you amused."

Feeling how hard he is, I grip it tightly. Sliding my hand up and down, I tease him. Probably a bad idea, but I'm gathering up all my bad ideas in one year. It was a bad idea to chase Crystal outside. It was a bad idea to taunt Busta at the warehouse, and it was definitely a bad idea to kill Nock. I might as well stack 'em up.

Bending down and covering my mouth with his, I taste the tang of his consumed beers. Tangling his tongue within, enjoying his war, I run my tongue along the edge of his teeth. Pulling back slightly, just enough to speak, I whisper, "If you get me alone, I might have to show you what this tongue can do beyond getting me in trouble."

"I think that would still be constituted as trouble, Obi."

"Well, you'll just have to find out."

Lifting me with a growl, he sets me on the back of his bike, then climbs on and starts us out of the lot.

Chapter

B<u>usta</u>

Heading out of town to my place, the roads are quiet. After the crazy busy, fucked-up day, I'm glad. I don't think I could handle soccer moms and assholes on phones.

Sitting at a light, waiting for it to turn, I give Obi's hand a squeeze. She's been holding my erection the whole time. Stroking it a few times, then using it as a handlebar, it's a great reminder that she hasn't fallen off. Also, that I'll be fucking her as soon as we enter the house. Seeing her behind that bar, watching her command the room with the brothers in my club, it felt right. She felt right. I felt at peace with her there.

Yeah, I was the bastard saying that I don't need a woman in my life. I was the bastard that said any of these fuckers that were strapped down with a bit of pussy, that it held them hostage—that they were trapped. I figured they were just asking for trouble in their lives. Yet here I am. She's shown me strength, compassion, and that she can hold her own with a bottle of Jack. She's damn near perfect.

"Almost home," I yell over the roar of my bike. I don't hear her reply, and as the light changes, I speed off.

Thinking about everything—King and his mess—our disaster, and how it's affecting all the surrounding clubs, I decide we need to step up our timeline. We need to beat him at his own game.

Getting home, I park in the garage. "I have a call I need to make. You go grab a drink, Obi. I'll be right in."

With a nod, she walks inside. I watch her retreating ass the whole time and think about how King is now not only causing issues in the club, and in my life at the club, but he's fucking with my sex life too. My once rock-hard cock that was ready to make Oubliette scream is subdued.

Grabbing a beer from the bar fridge, I close the garage and start walking to the back of the house along the side. The grass over here is a bit crunchy, and I'll remind myself later that the sprinkler timer should be dialed up.

Hitting the button for Death, he replies with a heavy grunt. "This better be good. I was knee-deep in pussy."

If mine's sidelined, only fair someone else's is on account of King.

"We need a meet, sooner rather than later." I don't want to say too much, as I'm not sure who's listening. There could be bugs, or someone in earshot.

"Tomorrow. Come to Humble." Without awaiting my answer, Death hangs up.

Dialing another, the phone doesn't connect immediately. Ring after ring, I wait. "What's up, Pres?"

Fuck, I still need to get used to that.

"Did you call your sister?" I ask.

"Yeah. She's got us a meet with Sinner and Soulless the day after tomorrow," Miss informs me, still slightly slurring his words.

"Push it up. Have them meet you and me at Humble Club tomorrow. Noon, I'll ride over with Oubliette."

"With Oubliette, huh?" His voice is full of mirth.

Fucker.

"Yeah, with the *bartender*. I'm sure Death would be happy to see she's safe."

Laughing into the phone, Miss has a hard time controlling his drunken giggles. "Fuck me."

"Shut it. Just meet me tomorrow at the club." Hanging up, I still hear his laughter. Asshole.

Pocketing my phone, taking in the darkness and the stars, the light leaves a reflection on the water below. Grabbing a seat on one of the chairs out here, I blow out the pent-up frustration that's been mounting. First with DG, then the brothers. Now I'm head of this shit, and I have a responsibility to the club to tell them the truth. They don't know about King. They don't know about all the shit that's happened and that continues because of Cruel Intentions and my past. Because of me and the choices I made then.

Yeah, King thinks he owns me—always has. Taking me from my family and invading my life all that time ago. He forgets, I was trained to be the asshole I've become.

He took the darkest parts of me to create the weapon he's hoping to use against those I care for now. I won't bow. I won't break.

Pulling out my wallet, taking out the small picture with worn corners, I look at it in the moonlight. The faces of the people that meant the most to me that lifetime ago, the people that I fought to protect that have fallen into memory.

I never gave in fully to King, never truly becoming his puppet, and I guess that's why I've excelled at the Bows. I'm my own man, and he's the same. Cody is just as strong, just as willful.

My little brother had disappeared from sight for years, until last year. I'd thought he'd found an out—a lucky life without club intervention. A pool in the backyard with football buddies and cheerleading short shorts. When I'd heard rumblings about a guy that looked like me, I had the boys investigate a new club in the area. With the answers I expected, my suspicions had been confirmed.

To fight this, to fix it, I know I'll need Cody and his club involved.

Using whores, intel, and cops on the take, I was able to grab his phone number. I hadn't called it yet, but it's time he and I had a chat.

Scrolling through my phone, thumbing the number, I press it.

"Hello?" His groggy voice carries across the small speaker.

"Cap."

"Yeah, who's this?"

"It's Lucius."

"Lucius? I don't know—"

"Yeah, you do. Now, I need you to listen, Cap." I don't know if this will push him, but I have to try. I have to try and break this secret wide open—I need to fix our lives.

"How the fuck did you get this number? No, better yet, what the fuck do you want calling me in the middle of the night?" Cap sounds just like our father. Same tone, and same patience too, I'll bet.

"I know you're in Orange County, brother. We need a meet."

"Not interested."

"This is about something bigger than a grudge. Do you know of the Humble Club?"

Cap replies, "Yeah. Why? That's Army run." His tone softens. He's listening at least. For now, that's the best I can ask for.

"Meet there tomorrow at noon. And Cap? Bring your VP."

"Like I'd come alone." With that, the line clicks as he hangs up, and I do the same.

"Fuck, I hope this works."

Chapter

B<u>usta</u>

Walking back in the house, I find Obi passed out on the living room couch. She's snoring lightly, drool dribbling out of her mouth, and damn near naked. Just looking at her is killing me. Her shirt is off, her jean shorts are on the floor. Her bra and flimsy underwear are the only things covering her. Poor woman hasn't had decent clothing in a week.

Fuck, I need to take her shopping. At the least, she needs to go to her condo to grab some things. Even though I *want* to enjoy her like this, because yeah, she's damn near perfect, I know I can't.

Walking over, I pick her up and move down the hall. Listening to her soft whine, I laugh. It entices me more and more to learn her little quirks, to find out what makes her tick.

Placing her in the bed and smiling, I tuck the blankets across.

"Thank you, love," she murmurs, curling in on herself.

Love.

I can't remember a time that anyone has called *me* 'love.' I've been asshole, fucker, cocksucker, and on numerous occasions, douche, but never *love*. Peeling off my cut, my shirt and my jeans, I curl into the bed beside her. Roping an arm around her chest, holding her boob as if it anchors me, I spoon her tiny body. Nothing feels more perfect.

I'm fearful of that.

What if what I'm doing will mess this up? Whatever this is, will it last?

King will fuck this.

No...*I'll* fuck this.

The shit thing is I have to. I have to make this right. I have to make it right for all of us.

No more hiding in the shadows, no more letting people run and ruin my life. I'll choose my fate, and I'll choose hers. We'll make this right for all.

Falling asleep, my mind drifts to the past and how it's blatantly fucking me over again.

Fucking King.

• • • •

"COME ON THEN. LET'S have a go. Show me your worst, Colton." Plowing his feet into the sand, kicking out his stance to make him that much harder to knock over, Colton knows his sheer size makes him a brute. He knows this is coming down to a fight and he thinks he's prepared. He deserves everything he's about to get.

The reason for the fight is simple. For years, Colton chased my sister. He wanted in her pants, and once he did, he unfortunately knocked her up in the process. Colton then turned tail and took off like a coward bitch. Today's the first day I've seen him in months.

For a guy that was here every day after school and before, whining and attempting to win her, to now shut down and leave without a word, it was noticed. Finding out my sister was pregnant, he ran. That didn't help matters.

He's left her to stress about this alone. Today is the moment his dad and mine had a long, drawn-out conversation about Dejene's future. That and the baby's future.

Our dad's a calm enough guy, up until the point you piss him off. When his baby girl thinks the only route out of a situation is to have an abortion because your ass doesn't want to assume responsibility, you best know how to run. Otherwise, if you're in the state of New York for more than a split second, he'll find you. Once he starts up that bike, you need to run, and run fucking fast.

My brother and I have been on the receiving end of his displeasure after bad grades, so I'd hate to be Colton's dad Marion, as he's being lectured about his son right now. He's probably having his ass handed to him.

Leaving my brother, me, a few of our friends and Colt alone, I couldn't be happier about it.

Sure, Colton has a good fifty pounds on me, at least six inches, and he's clearly all around bigger in every way, but I'm a cunning prick. Him grinding in his feet and preparing to fight me won't do him any good. I'll fix this the right fucking way.

That's me. I fix things. I don't let anyone get away with bullshit. I don't back down even when it's probably best I should, and I'm not afraid to get a bit bloody.

Not bad for a kid that's only turning seventeen next week.

I'm doing this my way.

"Colt, I don't give a flying fucking Harley if our dads work it out diplomatically for Dejene. I have an opinion on the outcome about you."

I don't need to look at my little brother, Cap. I know he's in full agreement. He's two years younger, but just as definitive on the matter as I am. Noticing him and our buddies, Rap, Johnson, and Joker beside me, I know the way this will go. There's no way I'm letting Colt walk out of this clubhouse without sustaining damage. Neither are they.

"Man, look. I'm not the only guy—"

"Really? You really wanna go there? Calling my sister a fucking whore to my face?" Cap pipes up jokingly, but with menace in his tone. He and my dad have that same tone. The same noise in their voice when they've reached the end of their patience. I notice as he steps closer, zeroing in on his target, ready to level him, but this is mine first and foremost. Cody, better known as Cap, is ready to break bones. Can't say I disagree, but I'm laying the first punch. He can bury the scraps.

Kicking out with my left leg, nailing Colton in the knee hard, I hear the bones crack. Busted.

He kneels on the ground, tears welling in his eyes, but I don't let up. Slamming a fist to his cheek, I love it as my bones rattle from the hard surface they hit. Hitting him hard under his chin, I feel a crack in his teeth as they crash together.

Spitting blood to the ground, still cradling that knee, Colton tries to stand. Pushing him by the shoulders, I keep him low. "You can't disrespect our sister on club grounds and expect we'll allow it. Turning away when you found out she's pregnant from your fucking filth-ridden cock is bad enough, but to blame her in any way is asking for you to leave without teeth." Pulling the pistol out of my waistband and pointing it at Colton's tiny, teeny, minuscule cock, I cock the hammer. "I hope you know how to suck cock, because when I'm done with you, your mouth will be your only asset left." Pushing it tight to his chest, I aim low to scare the punk. "Try me. Just give me one reason to not blast your fucking baby dick off?"

His look, that was once cocky, has greened a bit. "You okay, Colton? You look a little pale, like you've seen something scary." His eyes are trained on the gun in my hand, ready to blow his shit to pieces. Smiling, I think of how he'll have a lovely vagina by the time I'm done. Stepping a touch closer, bending low to face him, I place the point deep against his jeans, causing him to jerk slightly.

"What do you want from me?"

"Nothing anymore. We just want you to disappear for good." I think it's the right thing for everyone.

Looking at my brother, his devilish twitch glows with the mirth of his menacing thoughts. With a wink, I know what he has in mind. "Lu, let's show him what we do to assholes and cocksuckers that fuck with our family."

Peeling out his butterfly knife, Cap grins, and I swear I hear the gears in his mind turn. Laying it against Colton's throat, it tightens, and his Adam's apple bobs.

"I swear—"

Pushing the muzzle tighter brings me closer to the piece of shit.

"You probably swore undying love to Dee, but here you are, Colt. Trying to weasel your way out of a baby."

"It's not about the baby! Our dads aren't having a chat about that, you idiots!" Surprising me slightly, Colt rises up to his full height. Standing a little shorter with a busted kneecap, he blurts out, full of pride, "We know about you. I know about the club and what it's in to. Dad's only here trying to protect me—to keep me from doing something stupid." He smacks his chest a few times. "The cops will know everything. Do your worst, boys, and spend the rest of your lives in jail." Colt's backbone must be made of hardened fucking steel if he thinks he can damage our club. Especially after what he's done to our sister. And explaining his evil plan about cops and going to them with intel, he's the dumbest dumb guy for telling us if it's the truth.

Glaring hard into his eyes, I try to pull more info from him. I feign interest. It seems to be what he's hoping for. "What did you say, Colt?"

Pushing the knife away, he looks a bit bolder and less fearful. Funny part is, Cap seems a bit alarmed by the balls this kid shows too. "I have proof, I have protection. They told me that. They told me I'd be safe. With what my dad knows, they're protecting us."

"Who? Who's protecting you?" Smacking him across the face with the butt end of my gun, tears stream down his cheeks. Even as his boldness decreases, he still thinks he'll come out of this unscathed.

Inside, I'm fuming that this piece of shit thinks he has anything that could harm the Intentions. That he or his dad can cause us harm. "Listen, and listen good, Colt. Our family is untouchable. We own the cops in New York. We own the State for fuck's sake. So why do you all of a sudden have this urge of superiority?" Yeah, I've only just turned seventeen, but I know this piece of garbage can't do shit.

"They know where the kids go. They know you traffic across borders. They know all about you, assholes! That's why I'm here, that's why dad's here. We're your final nail in the coffin." And that's when I'd heard enough of his smug attitude. Pointing the gun upward at his throat, I feel the click and watch as shock shoots through his head. Well, that, and a nine mil bullet.

Fucker falls to the ground, his body sloppy and without power. Like a stringless marionette.

"Fuck! Jesus Christ, Lu! Why the fuck did you do that!" Cap shouts at me. "I just put on this clean shirt for fuck's sake! Mom's gonna murder us for the wash." Smoothing down his tee, that is now splattered with gray matter and blood, I shrug as I slip the gun back in the waistband of my jeans.

Joker and Rap are shell-shocked, standing but blinking slowly at the dead body that rests at their feet. I don't regret it...I don't regret it at all.

"We should go check in on Dad and make sure he knows what's coming," I tell them as I kick dirt on the face of Colton.

"What about the piece of shit?" Cap pipes up. "We can't leave it here. One of the kids could find it."

Starting away from the body, I head toward the clubhouse. "Fuck 'em. Let it rot." Not turning around to check that Cap and the boys are following, I add, "Just tell the kids there's a patch of Brussel sprouts and cabbage back here. They're afraid of that shit anyway."

Walking back into the clubhouse, immediately we know something big is going down. Wives and kids are running around, members are tossing paper into shredders, then lighting the remnants on fire in the sink by the bar. That fuck Colton wasn't lying. I probably shouldn't have shot him, but I'm not disappointed with the outcome.

Seeing my dad across the way, sitting at the bar, he looks calm and almost serene as he sips a cool glass of whiskey.

I nod to my brother and our friends. "Go see who needs help. I'm gonna chat with dad."

Walking over, leaving the boys to figure other shit out, I sit in the empty seat beside my father, Grim, the President of the Cruel Intentions.

My dad is one scary motherfucker to look at. At six foot, and almost as wide in the shoulders, with his long, dark, black beard twisted into two parts, stark gray eyes that I've sworn for years you could see a storm coming in—owned by a man who never smiles, he's a frightening fucker.

Breaking the silence, I ask, "I'm assuming you talked to Marion?"

Not looking my way, he raises his glass and sips the amber liquid before answering. "Yep."

"Where's Marion?"

"In church, with a bullet through his head."

"Fitting," I say, smirking.

Turning my way, finally, my single reply seems to have pulled him from the trance of brew and stew. "Fitting why?"

"Because his son is out behind the old parts shed with the same apparel."

Reaching over the bar, grabbing up the bottle that sat there lonely and asking to be drank, he pulls up another glass. Pouring me a shot, he settles it in my path. "You know, I'd hoped you were that kind of leader, son. I knew you could have the cool temper to see what needed to be done when it had to." Shrugging, he smacks me on the shoulder in a respectful way. "You'll be a great leader someday, Lucius. I know you will. Sorry fucking world, though, that I won't get to see it."

Pulling the glass to my mouth, downing a fair amount of the fire, I let it make its way to my soul—quenching the need to rain down further damage. The club's in trouble. We're in trouble if I understand it correctly. Killing the two snitches won't make a lick of difference to the club's outcome by the looks of it. We're going to have heat—and soon.

"What now? Not that I'm rushing things, but why is everyone running around, and we're sitting her calmly having a drink?"

Pouring another long shot, Dad seems at peace. He's too calm, honestly, and I'm frightened by it. There's more danger in him quiet than with him loud. "The DEA and State Police are just outside the compound. They'll be breaking down the door any minute. I figured, have a drink. It'll be a bit before I can breathe fresh air and drink a nice whiskey again. Might as well enjoy it."

Drinking down my own glassful, I rest back on the high-back stool. I have the feeling my life is about to turn deadly and crazy. Like Dad said, I might as well enjoy it while I can.

I guess I won't see the light for years either. I killed someone. I don't regret it.

Walking in like they own the joint, no less than a glass of whiskey later, DEA, State Troopers and city cops flood the club. Pointing, yelling, directing and arranging members and families into groups, Dad and I stay put. We don't turn to look, we know what's going on. The cops are rounding us up, and one by one, everyone is singled out in some way.

I can see the commotion from around the room in the mirror behind the bar. Certain members singled out, my sister brought into the room and gathered up with the other teenagers. The ladies and young girls are confused and seriously stressed out, whereas the young men and boys pretend to be stronger than they are against hardened law enforcement. That's when he approaches the bar.

Leaning across, reaching for a glass and the neck of the whiskey, my dad slams his hand against the bottle harshly as the newcomer tries to take it for himself.

"That's not for the likes of you." Seeing Dad's sneer as he tells off the man with a smug grin, the fancy prick releases the bottle.

Strutting behind the bar, selecting a bottle of rum, he pulls out the stopper and fills his glass. "It's nice to meet you, Hector. Or should I call you Grim? I mean, after all, your club is about to be disbanded. I guess I should call you Hector, right? You can't be a president of a pile of bones."

"It's Grim. What do you want, ya pig piece of shit?" It's not a request to answer what they want, it's a comment. One laced with disgust, disdain, and merciless hatred. I didn't notice if Dad was wearing his piece, but if he isn't, I am. This guy makes one false move and we'll rain down hell. I'd rather die taking him out than being held in a jail for the rest of my life anyway.

Wagging a brow, the only indicator that he's enjoying this more than he should, the stranger introduces himself. "I'm King. I'm here to close your shop up, old man. Time to say goodbye to the Cruel Intentions for good."

Refilling his glass, sipping it a few times, my dad is the epitome of calm. When he finally speaks, it's cool and without interest. "That'll be a sight to see. Our lawyer should have us all out in a few days."

"Decidedly not. You see, I have a trick up my sleeve, Hector." Calling over to a, Johnathan, the man turns our way and walks toward us.

Pulling up a chair, the new, fancy-suited prick takes a seat beside me. Nonchalantly, I give him a once-over. Not a tall guy by any means, not big either, but he exudes an air of superiority. In a pressed, dark blue suit, stark white tie, neatly combed low curls and burning blue eyes, he leans on the bar. "I'm Johnathan Hart. I'm here as the Homeland Security agent for this region, and unfortunately, you've violated quite a few of the rules that governs the US—your non-native country, Mr. Hector Guierra. As such, we are enacting our rights under the ICE program. You are to be immediately deported, turned over to the Mexican authorities—and I hear they will be immediately imprisoning you until a trial is set, based on racketeering, extortion, human trafficking, gun running, a litany of drug offences—and if you'd wish, I can continue with the slightly smaller infractions too."

Dad stays quiet as the smug asshole runs it all down. Slowly sipping, refill, sip and refill, without turning his eyes from the bottle that occupies his attention to the Government jerk, Dad is quiet. I'd always known my father wasn't a US citizen, but my mother is. He's never kept that a secret. I never thought that the government would come calling to deport him, though. He's lived here for over twenty years. Sure, he's not a law-abiding citizen, so I doubt he can do anything to change that outcome with a lawyer. This has been well-thought-out, I'll bet.

"So, you turn me over. So what? I'll be back in no time. Or if not me, the Cruel Intentions will be. You can't keep a good club down. We're all

law-abiding citizens here. The charges you've just listed are unfounded, debasing, and without merit. You won't be able to make even one stick."

Pulling away from the ledge he was leaning on, taking a phone out of his pocket, King plays a video. "They know where the kids go. They know you traffic across borders. They know all about you, assholes! That's why I'm here, that's why Dad's here. We're your final nail in the coffin." It's Colton's voice, just before I shot his brains out.

"I think we might differ on that rate of return for your club. Either it's done, or your son here spends his days in a jail far from here, without protection, without assistance, and without a way out." He places his phone back in his pocket, "Now I do have a second recording of a meet from the office down the hall there, and I'm sure it reflects what happened to Marion George while your son was finishing off his son outside."

Dad doesn't say anything, but his face darkens. There's an ashen, fearful, worried appearance—that's a look I've never seen. Sucking down the last of his glassful, Dad slides the glass across the bar where it clinks with the bottle.

He rises from the chair. "Let's go talk, King."

"After you," he says smugly as he walks behind my father.

While they start away, the fancy pants dressed dude places a hand on my arm. "You and I need to stay here."

"Fuck you. You aren't my father. I don't have to listen to your shit."

Grasping my arm tight, slinging it behind me, he presses my face into the bar. Latching a pair of cuffs on, I squirm as he clicks them in place. "Enjoy that feeling for a minute. If your father and King don't have a solid agreement, you'll be leaving here with me, boy."

Lifting my head, I spit on his pristine suit. "I'm not your boy. I'm no one's fuckin' boy."

Wiping down the mess with a towel off the bar, and grabbing the gun from between my waistband and shirt, he uses the towel to pull it away. He's being awfully careful not to wreck any prints. Winking, he grins smugly. "We'll disagree, kid. In the end, though, I'll fucking win."

Calling someone over to hand him a bag, he sets the gun inside it with a smile. He knows he's holding the instrument of my long-term visit with the correctional facilities.

"Not as tough as you think." Sealing up the bag and setting it in the man's hands, I watch as he wanders off to a collection area to set it with other pieces being logged by a fat bitch in a DEA vest. With a cool look over here, disdain is written on her face.

She's not who I'm most interested in, though. Those deep brown eyes, rimmed in hatred and disappointment. She's beyond mad. Seething. Cradling the head of my sister in her lap, stroking her fingers through her soft curls, my mother is trying to soothe Dejene. Her eyes tell me the story. Sorry won't cut it to get out of this. I'm more sorry than I can say, Mama.

"She seems pissed at you, kid."

I grind my teeth. "I'm not your kid. I'm not your son, I'm not your bro, and I sure as fuck don't give a shit what you think."

"Lucius!" my mother crows. "Respect." Her eyes narrow, scolding me. "Have respect, even when they don't."

God, I love my Mama. Even when we're dealing with the law, danger, and potential jail time for all, she's worried about decorum and manners.

"Sorry, Mama." Laying my head on the bar with a thunk—harder than I'd hoped—I button my mouth and sit still.

Even as commotion surrounds myself and the agent, I shut up. Mama said to shut it, and I did. I don't wish her ire. I'd almost rather jail than to piss her off.

After what feels like hours, as I rest my head and keep my trap shut, eventually my dad walks out of the back with the man named King. "Lucius."

Sitting back on the stool, resting against my hands, I perk up at the mention of my father saying my name. Standing at my side, looking down on me with a pinched, sorrowful gaze, he states, "This is something I can't fix."

Chapter

B<u>usta</u>

Waking with a start, the last words of my father still ring heavily in my head.

This will be a disastrous day. I feel it. I feel it so deep in my bones that every nerve itches and my skin feels alight. With my arms still wrapped around Obi, I feel sweaty and overheated. Everything can go wrong. Everything.

If I fuck this up, there's so many people that will be ruined with it. This happened once before with the Cruel Intentions, and the guilt of it is crushing again. The weight of it on my shoulders feels like a building collapsing. It's awkward and disgusting. To think, this all happened because of my relationship with King.

A few weeks back I was still the DEA informant, snitch, mole, whatever the fuck you want to call it, but I was also a Broken Bow that followed orders, that felt I was surrounded by a team of men that I trusted—that trusted I was a Bow through and through, and that I'd follow the club rules as holy writ. That was until her. Until I saw her in that club. Until I'd been asked to sit her sorry ass. Until I'd...

Until I fell for her.

True set me with the task of dragging info from her about the Army, and in turn, set me in her path. Now I'm wrapped up in her arms, truly satisfied to stay there all day, to avoid our fate. To avoid the fate that can go terribly wrong. This must go right, not only for her, me and the clubs, but for my family and everything that destroyed us.

King had set up the club. For a long time, the club thought that they were untouchable, that they were beyond the law. It was King. He told me that. There was nothing in our control. Now that it was affecting me and my family, I saw it firsthand. I was also informed that if I wished to save the membership from Children's Aid, jail terms—though he couldn't save them all—that I'd have to cooperate. Dad too.

Stepping into church, the body of Marion was covered with a towel. The stain of his blood leeched into the carpet, but his head—or what was left of it—was covered by the green and gold towel.

"Have a seat, kid," King instructs.

Again, another fucker thinking I'm their kid. They don't have the right to treat me as such. Good fucking luck.

"I'll stand, thanks."

Shutting the door to the inner sanctum, that I'd only seen peeking through the partially opened door, standing here feels prohibited. I don't have a right to be here as an unpatched member of the Cruel Intentions. Then again, this fucker and his agent friend shouldn't be in here either as far as I'm concerned. I shut my trap, though, and wait for Dad to tell me what the fuck is going on.

Taking a seat at the head of the table, King knowingly takes the position of power. Pulling out a chair beside him, he taps it. "Have a seat, Hector. Let's give a rundown to your son on his new job." The smarmy look on King's face tells me this is something I'm going to despise. As his buddy takes the seat beside my dad, he motions for me to have a seat across the table.

"Lucius, sit." Without his usual growl and gruff demeanor, Dad's tone is apologetic and subdued. Imploring me with his eyes, I relent and take a seat.

Rubbing his hands together, then smacking them, King starts. "So, Lucius. You're a young lad. Strong-willed too, I suppose, and I think you and I can come to an agreement on something that can benefit the many."

"I doubt it."

"See, this is where you're wrong. I know you can." Smiling, King looks to both of us. "Let me break it down for you. Dear ol' Dad is being deported. He'll be handed to the Mexican authorities, and he'll be imprisoned until he's shanked in jail. The rest of your family will be torn to pieces. Cody will be sent to juvie, Children's Aid for your sister, and a somewhat comfortable jail—in the case of your mother. That will *be for aiding, abetting, and the other charges that your dad has, but as accessories to the fact. Light and freedom will not be theirs. Oh, and your sister, Dejene, will never see the face of that babe. An abortion will be swiftly conducted." With King stating this so callously, Dad rises from his chair. King doesn't look his way. "Have a seat, Hector. We haven't gotten to the best part."*

"Motherfucker, you promised! No fuckin' way will something like that happen to my baby girl." My Dad will rip the roof off this building and rain down hell if they think someone will harm her or that child. They've really pissed him off. Does it make me insane if I want to see him kill these agents with a gavel?

Waving off Dad's anger, King continues. "So, as I was saying, that is what can *happen. But it's up to you, Lucius."*

"What do you want from me?"

"We're recruiting."

"Then go grab yourself a team of little robots that tow the company line. You lost two informants today with Marion and Colton. Poor souls. Killing themselves was awful. Suicide is not the way to go." I'm sarcastic and dangerously close to probably pissing these guys off, but I don't care.

"Yes. It is sad. So, here's the proposal, and you only get one shot at it. Accept it, or take door number two, the door that will ruin your family. Ready?"

Grinding my teeth, I zip it as I wait for his proposal.

"You're gonna come work for me. You'll volunteer, naturally, and you'll excel at it. Top student, passing with flying fucking colors, and you'll become our top guy. If you do, I'll put your family in safer places than jail. Get me? You become one of us and help me do what I need. Johnathan here has already approved it. He'll make sure your father stays in the US—in a maximum-security prison, in solitary. Your mom will be sent to live with relatives in Colorado or some other shit state, and your sister and brother will be relocated to unknown locations to live freely and without persecution until they hit age of majority. They fuck it up on their own

after that and it's on them, but until they do, they're my responsibility. That's the deal. They walk, the club closes shop and doesn't reopen, and you become a DEA agent for me. Simple. Easy peasy.

"You hold up your end of the bargain and do everything as a model fucking guy, or they end up in the hellholes that they should've been in all along." Resting back in the president's chair, he's altogether too comfortable in that seat. He's blackmailing my family and me into servitude. I can't believe it, and I don't understand why.

I ask, "Why me?"

"Well, honestly, I've been watching you for a year. You're tough, you're a cunt that takes no shit from anyone. Your knowledge of club life can assist us. You'll do a fabulous job of being a fucking asshole in our infiltration division. You're exactly what I need." Crossing his arms, King is dangerously content with himself.

He isn't giving me much of a choice. All I have to trade is myself to the DEA.

"I guess I have no choice."

Smacking his hands together and gathering up the gavel, he raps it on the plate. It rattles my teeth and makes me want to make him eat the most religious part of my life. I want him to shit slivers.

Standing, King grins. "Glad you're joining the team." Starting toward the door, King turns to Johnathan. "Have Lucius sign his paperwork. Make sure Hector signs off too as a willing participant, and we'll get this show on the road."

Stepping out into the hallway, King disappears, leaving me in the care of my father, who looks worn-out, and Johnathan and two other DEA agents, who seem stoic and disconcerted with the process.

He slides some papers across the table. "You'll need to sign this."

"Sure. How do I sign with my hands behind my back? Stupid cunt."

Cocking his head sideways, clearly not impressed with my smart response, Johnathan motions for one of the other officers to uncuff me.

Rubbing my wrists after the cold bracelets are gone, I look at the paperwork set before me. There's at least twenty pages, full of jargon and shit I don't get, and it only has one spot to sign. Not wasting time reading through something I don't understand, I lift up the pen and sign it, then push it across the table to the jerk's awaiting hands. "Here. Just promise they're all safe."

"As safe as we can make them," he says coolly. I wonder how dangerous this is, how badly I've signed my life over to the devil, or if I'm trading one prison for another.

"Will I get a copy of that?" I ask him.

"Yeah. You can read it as a bedtime story after training."

My dad picks up the pen, signs beside my name, as well as signing other paperwork they toss at him, then deflates slightly. The strong, dangerous president is now a ward of the judicious system.

None of this should be legal. Yes, this totally goes against the right to lawful proceedings, but we've signed over our lives because we have no other choice. This is do or die. This is be or be nothing. I'll be damned if I'm anyone's nothing.

Leaving that meeting, feeling—no, knowing I'd signed over my life to the government I despise, that I've always been told to reject, there's a deep pit in the bottom of my stomach that aches. Will I rail against this? Will I find a way out of this? You bet your ass I will. It could take me years, or fucking days, but at some point, I will find a release from this.

It only took the agents a few hours to round everyone up. Sending each on their intended paths, they clear out the dead and I sit there, watching families torn apart. Thankfully, they gave me a chance to say goodbye to my sister and brother, but my parents were taken away quickly. The agents didn't want a hassle from our parents. Their voluntary incarceration had to be done quickly, so they left nearly as quick as the ink dried.

At that age, I didn't really get what had happened. I knew I was saving others the fate we had, but my parents had pled guilty and no contest as they were led away. My brother was taken by a team of agents, our best friends were taken elsewhere, and as they fought the removal from the only place they'd known, it was depressing. The hardest part for me was my sister escorted out with a medic. Not with family. She was stressing over the whole thing. She attempted to kill herself in the bathroom when left alone for a moment.

That signature was exactly what I'd signed to not have happen. My family was destroyed.

The warm body beside me is a great reminder that I had something to fight for again after all these years. If I were given the chance to do it all over again, could I? No. I wasn't prepared to live a life in jail. King was saving me in a way. I don't appreciate it, and I still hate him for it in every way, but he did do something that was right for the seventeen-year-old me.

I vowed then that I would find a way to bring down King. Now with it in my grasp, I can taste it. The bitter tang of revenge is sitting heavily on my tongue. He's cocky, he's glib in his position of power. He's used the wars between the clubs to his advantage. He's not expecting us to rally. King, in his smug way, won't expect us to work it out.

He doesn't expect his *well-trained* pet to rebel.

Stirring slightly, Obi curves her ass along my hips.

"There's sunshine. Why is there sunshine?" Tucking the blanket above her head, it hides her sweet muffled sound. "Make it go away."

Pulling me from the murderous rage I was simmering toward, Obi's sweet disappointment with the light is humorous. Could I stay here all day? Yes.

I can be late.

I can show up fashionably late.

"The sunlight is inevitable in California. You can't avoid it," I tell her jokingly.

Raising a hand, she slams it against my mouth. "Stop talking. Your voice is too loud. God, why do guys have to sound like a tractor when you just want quiet hangovers?"

Laughing through her fingers, I decide that quiet isn't what I want. Licking her finger, lifting my head slightly, I suck her finger into my mouth.

"Oh, come on." She pouts. "Hangovers don't go away when you do that."

I release her finger. "Maybe you've never had the right guy waking you when you've had a hangover." Pulling her hips closer, flicking the edge of her thin panties, I yank on them, feeling the soft material give.

"Did you just break one of the last pieces of clothing I have left to wear?" Her dark tone isn't sinister. Oubliette is about as dark and sinister as a rainbow covered unicorn riding on a cloud owned by talking donuts and sparkly dogs.

"I have a theory." Running a hand down her hip, delving within her heat, my cock pokes into her backside as I enjoy her warmth.

"You do?" She wiggles her hips back and forth. "I don't think you have a theory. I don't think you're a planner. I think you're a fly-by-the-seat, go-with-the-flow kind of guy, Lucius." Reaching her hand around, she grasps my stiffening cock. "Or do you plan to cause mayhem and destruction?"

Hitting that on the head, she's damn near exact in her assessment.

"I plan mayhem and destruction. From experience, just *flying by* has caused me a world of hurt." Rocking within her hand, feeling the softness of her grip, I can tell she's fearful of her grip being too tight. I cover her tiny one with mine. "You can't hurt me. Not like that."

"How can I hurt you then?" She means it in a playful way, but with the reminders of family and what I've lost, I take it completely different.

Turning her body to face me, Oubliette's starry, beautiful eyes request an answer. "Break my heart."

She smiles. "If anyone's going to get a broken heart here, it's me. I've taken a risk. I think I've taken *all* the risks so far. Stolen after seeing a murder, murdering someone who tried to cause me harm, taken hostage—again, set under a microscope at a clubhouse, got in a fight with a kitten at said club, and now it seems I'm stuck in something that has nothing to do with me because of my job and *club business.* It's all been about club business. I think the person who has the biggest risk here is me. Hearts are the least of our worries."

Taken aback by her glib reply, I know it's going to put an abrupt stop on my sex this morning, but it has to be said. I'm not one for letting things lie. "Cynic much?"

"Sometimes." Kissing my forehead, she rises out of bed. "I mean, honestly. I'm not your girl—not in the true sense. You didn't date me. You didn't take me out for a fancy dinner to get to know me before kidnapping me, so excuse me if I'm sarcastic about my role that I play in this fiasco." She looks around the room. "Where are my shorts? The least you can do is let me wear something as I walk out of here."

Flinging shirts, my jeans, and finally stepping into the bathroom to look, Obi is concerned about leaving my house in a naked state. I'm not, because she's not without me as her escort. That was the point. I don't intend on her leaving this house alone. Yes, I'd mentioned that she was going to the meet with me, but not without clothing.

Tossing off the covers and grabbing up my jeans, I sling them on, as well as a fresh shirt. "Feel free to watch whatever it is you'd like. The fridge is stocked and the hangover should be enough of a deterrent to stop you from emptying the liquor cabinet." Washing up and starting toward the garage, I still hear her tossing the room for her shorts. She won't find them. Before I slung her in bed, I took all of her clothing and hid them in the garage. My pants are excessively big on her tiny frame, even with those sexy as fuck hips, and I don't know many women other than whores that will walk around without panties. Color me tickled and sufficiently surprised if she will.

Pulling the door to the garage, Obi pops out of my bedroom, storming down the hall. "What do you expect me to do here, Lucius?

Play house? Hang out and wait for you to return? All because you stole my underwear and shorts?"

She stomps past me, heading into the garage.

"Where do you think you're going?" I ask with a wide smile.

Picking up a helmet off the workbench, she slings it on and stands by my bike, wearing nothing but a Bows T-shirt she's pulled from the drawer. "You rip my clothes, steal my shorts, and think you can leave me to wander in your home while you ride away? Nope. I'll ride naked if I have to." She takes the helmet off. "Fuck it. I'll walk or hitchhike. Naked should get me somewhere. I'm going to my house to grab something to wear, *Busta,* and you," she huffs, poking me in the chest, "are taking me."

What a sight. Obi's naked, if not for the shirt. The shirt lies just past her thighs, and it would stretch farther if it wasn't for those lovely hips and ass, but the white material leaves no imagination as to what's under it. "You're not riding naked, Obi. I have somewhere to be that doesn't involve this shit."

"I'm going with you. You don't get a choice. Hangover and all, I'm your problem today. Let's go."

"No," I say sternly.

Crossing her arms directly above that perfect set of tits, she starts to jump across the seat.

"You're not riding my bike naked."

"I'm not," she mocks while putting the helmet across again, and doing up the chin strap.

"You're right. You're not," I say, though if I'm being brutally honest, I think this is hot as fuck.

"I'm not naked. I'm wearing a shirt, Busta."

"Close enough," I mutter. "Look, you're naked. There's more seen than not." Stepping in her space, I reach out through the shirt and tweak a nipple. "You're not naked—not yet, but damn well close enough, Obi." Shit, I shouldn't have done that. My cock knows by autonomic responses that touching that milky white skin is a bad idea. Her rosy nipples call to me. My semi relaxed member is back awake and ready to fuck her until she relents. Until she passes out and I leave here without her.

Lifting the hem of the shirt, brushing her skin as I do, a sharp intake of breath escapes her. Still wearing that helmet, it turns me on further. One thing I've never done is take a woman on my bike. I've never fucked a woman on it, as none have been worth it.

Raising her up, setting her on the bike, she grins, thinking she's won. Removing the chin strap, I pull the helmet off. "Stay still," I tell her. Laying her across the seat so her back bows against the tank, I raise the shirt.

"Lucius—" She starts her protest until my mouth connects with her exposed clit. "Jesus Christ!"

Pressing her body tight to the seat, I hold her hostage once more. She's held in a sexual trance as I pull her greedy need from her. Her body is content to let me wreck it, to destroy it for any man that came before me, because no one will come after. I own her now.

No one else will.

I won't give her up to anyone.

Nothing can make me release her.

I may not have thought that earlier, but now that the idea is settled in my mind, it's finite. Nothing can change it.

Squealing with delight, she grips the handlebars behind her head, shoving her body closer to my mouth, directing me to her needs. Not like I need a road map to a woman's body, but I'm laughing inside that she tries. When I think she's had enough, that she's close to the edge, I relinquish my hold on her. Dragging her off the end of my bike, I sling her over my shoulder and walk inside the house once more.

"What the fuck! Lucius, finish what you started! We know how this goes. I'll do it without you," she complains hoarsely. Her voice hasn't become any closer to the sound she had before Nock, and I'm satisfied with that. She's sexy as fuck, and that voice makes her the most beautiful thing on this planet. If I'm being greedy, I don't fuckin' care.

Walking through the door, laying her back on her feet, I place her in front of the couch. "Hold that thought."

Reaching into my wallet and pulling free a condom—we've tempted fate a few too many times for me to do it again—I strip off my jeans and wrap up at the speed of light. Bending her over the couch back, raising her ass in the air, I toss the shirt away. "You can scream now."

Thrusting within her, Obi's tight pussy accepts and clamps around me as I shift back and forth. The feel of her is addictive, something I could stay inside of forever. Reaching around, grasping those soft globed tits, I pinch the pink tips that call to me. Her raspy voice growls as she whines with my moves and as my speed increases.

That long hair of hers tickles my abs as I move, begging for me to hold it. Releasing a handful of tit, I grasp her strands. Weaving it around my palm, her head is instinctively thrust backward. I lean forward as her body tightens toward her end. "Come for me," I growl in her ear.

"Not yet," she argues. Her body disagrees even as she tries to hold herself off. Screaming out her release within seconds, her inner walls tighten so harshly, I can't hold off. Rolling her hips to meet mine, I push hard against her body, growling out my own end.

"Fuck," I groan as the tightness subsides and Obi slouches against the couch.

Relinquishing her hair, kissing her on the back of her shoulder and easing myself out, I laugh as her body gives me back my cock. Pulling off the used wrapping, I tie it up, then walk it to the trash.

Oubliette falls forward across the leather, landing on the cushions with a lazy slap. "Wow. That was better than before. What will you do for an encore?"

"I have to leave, Obi." I know it'll start a new round of 'you're not going,' but I have to leave. It's eleven now, and I'm expected at Humble shortly. As it is, I'll have to speed like a motherfucker to get there on time.

Popping her head up from the couch, I can see the disappointment on her face. "Really? You're really looking to leave without me, still?"

"Oubliette—"

"You can't leave me here alone." Her tone changes. "I can't be alone yet. Please."

Noting how her voice sounds fearful, I blow out a heavy breath. I thought she was just looking to leave because she didn't want to be left here and left out. I forget that she's a strong woman—not needy and whiny. I keep forgetting that she's been through so much, and it must still be taking a toll.

"I don't have anything that will fit you, Obi."

"A pair of boxers until you can stop at my place. Or a store will do fine too." Stepping away from the couch, she walks up to me. "Please. With you, I'm with someone who understands what's in my head day in and day out."

"Obi—"

Placing a hand on my face, she strokes my beard and smiles. "Please. All I see is Nock's face, and it won't go away."

I kiss her on the forehead. "Give me a sec." Turning down the hall, walking to the back bedroom, I head into the closet. The closet holds old clothing that I hadn't gave to the charity company yet. Picking out a sweater and a pair of shorts with a tie, I walk back out. "Here." I hand her the clothes. "We need to get going."

Smiling, and pulling my head down for a kiss, Obi doesn't waste any time in tossing on the clothing. "Thank you."

Chapter

Oubliette

Rounding the corner, approaching the downtown core, I'm thankful that we're closing in on Humble. Sitting at a light, Lucius told me we were on our way to a meet. I'm glad we'll be someplace I feel at home, even if it means being around bad reminders.

I haven't been back at Humble since this all occurred, and I know it will be dangerous to my psyche, but I'm not one to shy away from fear. Driving his bike to the back of the club, pulling it alongside a row of neatly lined up others that are already in attendance, I hop off as he parks. Handing him the helmet, I start toward the rear entrance out of habit, forgetting I don't have my keys. I stop dead at the sight of the stain from Crystal. I don't notice as Lucius comes up behind me. "You okay?"

"I have to be." I'm short on options. Either I deal with the issue and overcome it, or I let it crush me.

As Lucius starts to the stairs, taking them two at a time, his heavy boots clack on the open grates. Following him up, I yell ahead, "I don't have my key."

"Don't worry, Death left it open. The front's locked and the bar's closed."

Making our way down the darkened hall, coming up on the staff room, I stop. "I'll meet you inside in a bit. I have a change of clothes in here."

As Lucius is almost past the stripper change room, he turns. "You sure?"

"Yeah, I'm fine. I need to wash up and get dressed in something that feels familiar." Pulling on the sweater, I think he takes the hint I need to wear something other than an old motorcycle shop logo sweater.

Walking back to me, he stands close enough that his breath brushes my face. "If you need me, yell out."

"Yeah, sure. I'm good. Go. You have a meet." I try to sound convincing and smile as big as I can, hoping it looks real.

Walking down the hall, leaving me to my own devices, Lucius heads toward the front. Once he's out of sight, I enter the staff area. The quiet of it is daunting. I'm used to a room that's hopping with a flurry of activity as guys come and go, waitresses are bitching about tippers and strippers, and bikers check up on their girlfriends. Unlocking my locker, I'm more than glad that I keep a spare set of clothing here. Pulling it out, along with my shower caddy and deodorant, I head to the showers.

Laying my clothes out, I'm almost excited. Soft materials, a clean bra set, jeans, and thankfully a spare set of trainers. I pet them, excited to step out and trash the shoes I've been wearing. Too many reminders, too many thoughts that bring me back to the activities as of late.

Stripping down, then turning on the shower and staying away from mirrors—because I haven't had a chance to put on makeup or do my hair nice for weeks—I get to work on feeling like Oubliette once more.

Chapter

B<u>usta</u>
Explaining a bit of it to Death earlier in the week at the hospital, I know it wasn't enough to prepare him for the events of today.

Leaving Obi at the back, I badly wanted to stay with her. I know she can look after herself, and that this is probably one of the safest places for her, but I still don't like leaving her. Thing is, this has to be dealt with. Nothing else matters at the moment.

Passing through the hall to the main area in the club, I see that everyone is here already. They're not sitting together and chatting like friends, but they're in the same room. That's a start in my opinion.

At a large table sits Death, another guy, and Miss. His VP Curse is missing, but I heard he's still hanging in there and getting better by the day. Obi was glad to hear it as Curse, she'd mentioned, was one of her favorite guys. Instead, seated beside Death is a very large guy and an oversized dog resting at his feet. It's one of those reddish-colored dogs like from that movie with the cop and the dog who's a witness to a crime. I can't remember the name of it, but this dog is just as big, slobbery, and dangerous looking.

At the second table sits Soulless and Sinner from the Heartless Bastards. Checking their phones and sipping on the beers in front of them, they raise their eyes as I walk in. I wouldn't expect anything less, as the last time I'd seen either of them, I was one of the few that had tried to do them damage—on directives from True.

The last table is the one I worry about and fear the most—the SoCal Soulless. Cap and Raptor stare me down with hate in their eyes. Murder in their intentions. I can't say I'm disappointed, as I'd be surprised if they didn't.

Rising from the table, Death yells out, "Busta! Good. Now we can get this show on the road." Pulling a beer from a bucket on the table, he uncaps it and hands it to me.

Starting toward him, but still not taking my eyes off Cap, I answer him. "Thanks, man."

"Where's my bartender?" Death asks, grabbing my attention. His smile is bright, quirky, and I can't blame him. She's damn amazing.

"In the back. She needed a shower and clean clothes." Taking the offered drink, the cool liquid flows freely and joyfully down my throat. Chin raising my newly appointed VP, Miss grins. He's already attached the VP rocker on his cut, even though my enforcer patch is still on mine. It's been a fucking whirlwind, and I haven't had the time to change it out. That, and my original vest houses a bullet from Death's sister. It's crazy how fast this shit has gone down. It's not been years, but weeks.

"Without sounding kinda crazy, tell me that guy looks pretty much like you." Death looks to Cap and mutters in a low tone.

Pulling the bottle away from my mouth, I wipe the foam from my lips. "Yeah, he definitely does." Setting the bottle down, I decide it's best to get any questions out of the way now. "Let's get to intros then."

"Sounds good, brother. We have a ton to discuss." Clasping his hand, I turn to my VP. "Miss, you good?"

He hasn't torn his eyes away from Cap, and I can just imagine the thoughts running through his head. We don't associate normally with guys from the south, as it crosses too many clubs. At least that was under DG. With me at the helm, I'm crossing that line. I need to for my own peace of mind.

Raising his voice slightly, he directs his comment at Cap and Raptor. "Would you mind coming over to this table? We've got enough room to seat us all."

With Death and his buddy rising, Miss moves to sit closer to his sister's beau. They've met a few times, and yeah, he wasn't happy at first with his twin dating a guy from another club, let alone their VP, but he'd been pretty cool about it after they met. Sinner is darker than I am, with no facial hair, and his head shaved tight to his scalp. With a multitude of tattoos that run along his throat, I assume they run down his body. Clothed, I can't see much more than what's showing, but he's definitely covering the real estate he has visible.

Soulless and I have met a few times. As enforcer, it was a part of the business. We've not been on the best of terms, but then again, who is when you're entering and messing with each other's territory or business? With a long scar down his forearm, Soulless holds it out for a handshake. "Busta. Congrats on the change in leadership. I hope this is a change for the good."

I shake the offered hand. "You and me both." I nod my head toward his VP. "Sinner," I greet as he eyeballs me. Under any other circumstances, we'd be guns drawn and blood spilt, but this is a change in the dynamics, a way to create something that will close off King from the game he plays with all of us. We're a ton smarter than he thinks, and it's time we showed him. Me calling him for an exit with Obi was a dumb move if I wanted to stay out of his way and under the radar, but it also started something that I can't staunch the flood of.

As Cap and Rap walk over and take a seat silently, I decide it's best to start. "I know this is your house, but do you mind if I do the intros, Death?"

"Nah. Go for it." Still looking from me to Cap, he has a driving need to find out who and what Cap is to me.

"Left to right, club to club. I'm Busta, newly appointed Pres of the Broken Bows, and this big bastard beside me is Single Miss. If he looks chummy with the man beside him, Sinner, it's because his sister is dating him." With a chin raise, he sucks back on his beer. "He's VP to the Heartless Bastards, and next on the left is his Pres, Soulless. Death, owner of this fine piece of pussy establishment, is Pres of Hade's

Army, and seeing his VP Curse is still in the hospital, he's in attendance with—" I pause, requesting the man to give us his name.

Death smacks his friend on the shoulder. "This is Trigger, and the dog is Radish. Trigger doesn't talk much. Don't expect a long, drawn-out conversation."

Fine by me. "Then the last two joining us are Captain and Raptor, his VP. The SoCal Soulless are from Orange County. The reason that he looks familiar is that Cap is my little brother. Long story. I won't get into it right now, fellas."

"Why?" Cap pipes up. "They might as well know you deserted your family, ran off with a DEA agent and left everything you ever knew in New York. I mean, why would that be a long story? I think that was pretty fucking short."

"Cap—"

"Don't fuckin' 'Cap' me, Lucius. I've waited years to hear this story, might as well draw it out as long as you can. After all, story or no story, truce or not, I'm putting a bullet in your skull once we walk out of here." He's deadly serious, and it puts Miss on alert.

I place a hand on Miss's shoulder. "It's good, brother. Let me run it all down before we start with the killing."

"Cap, I don't know you. I don't know shit about you and Busta, but I know who we're up against. If Busta can shed some light on it, more than he and I have already chatted on, then I'm open for discussions. You might want to give him a moment before that bullet flies. For your club, just as much as I'm doing this for mine." Death is calm, and as serious as a heart attack. His tone brokers no room for blood in his club.

"Your club, your rules, for the moment." Cap leans back in his chair. "Expect splatter marks on the pavement, though."

Taking a seat, I run down what happened the day I left Cruel Intentions. How the death of Colton and his father wasn't what killed the club, but King. That fucker took everything from me that day, even so much as my brother too. We were thick as thieves, and King has made us enemies. I'm hoping this sorts shit out.

"I know King has approached all the clubs in the area in some way. He's infiltrated them, setting his own men in places of power." Keeping a close watch on my brother as I run down the last ten plus years, I tell him everything. The training, the deal that was struck, and the way that King has kept us all in check. "There's no reason for you to trust me, and there's no reason for you to believe me, but we need a resolution to this. If we want to survive, if we want to take him down so that we can run our clubs the way we want, then we need to do this right."

As everyone settles into a quiet calm, thinking over everything I've told them, Oubliette walks out of the back. Wearing a thin, short, see-through tank top that shows of her midsection, a red bra—that hardly hides those nipples, tight black jeans that hug her curves in all the right spots, and a set of black heels, my concentration on the table wains. Fuck, she's damn gorgeous.

"Bennett!" she yells, running across the space.

Rising out of the chair, he hugs her tightly, murmuring into her hair, "Damn, girl, you lost weight. Those fucking hips are sticking out."

"Did I?" Only days have passed, but it's taken its toll on her. Being with her, as she wore the same clothing, I guess I never noticed the change. I never saw that she hadn't eaten much, that she hadn't been taking care of herself. Fuck. And I promised Death I would make sure she was good.

Looking over his shoulder at me, while he still has her wrapped in his arms, his scowl says the same. He's pissed. I think she looks fucking hot, but I don't see the difference that he does.

"Oubliette, have you been looking after yourself?"

Pulling back slightly, she smiles. "I guess not. You want a special?"

Deflection.

"Damn straight I do. Give me an Oubliette special. One for each of these men too." Taking his seat again, Death stares me down. "We'll chat."

Standing beside me for a moment, Obi touches my shoulder and says hello to Miss as she walks off to the bar. Watching as she walks in those heels, I make a mental note to have those wrapped around my head tonight.

"Damn. That's a nice piece of ass, Busta," Rap jokes. "Hate to see anything happen to that old lady. Hate to see her leave you for a real, *honest* man."

Spinning away from checking her out, I level Raptor with a glare. "You fucking think to touch that woman and I'll leave your bones on the pavement, *Jerry*."

Smirking, he raises his hands in mock defeat, but I know better. Even after all this time has passed, I know that Rap wouldn't worry about crossing a line between a brother and his girl.

Scowling at Raptor and giving me a look that states to leave it, Death speaks up. "Getting back to the business at hand, we need to set this up in our favor." Pulling another beer from the bucket in the middle of the table, Death uncaps it and waits for us to continue.

"I have an idea, but it takes all of us. We need to work it right."

"And how do you suggest that, Busta? King has his filthy fucking mitts in everything the clubs do. Everything. He has from the start, and he won't bother to worry about his pets when the fallout hits. We'll all go down." Cap thinks I betrayed him, that I betrayed the club. That I ran for higher ground when shit went down. Even with me telling him what happened, he still doesn't believe me. Fine, I'll show him the only way I know that can prove it.

Dragging out my phone, I play a recording, showing a middle-aged man receiving head from a *very* underage girl. It shows the back of his graying hair, the receding hairline that's just visible, and the view of her tied to a pole with his hands holding her in place. "Suck it hard. I don't care if you gag. I love it even more. Harder, harder," he yells at her, bringing her so close there's no way she can gasp for air. Yelling over his shoulder for someone, the man's face comes into view.

"Jesus fucking Christ! Is that who I think it is?" Cap looks at me, then at Rap, knowing we've seen that fucker before.

"Yeah, that's Director of Homeland Security, Johnathan Hart. The dude who was there when we were taken down in the Cruel Intentions. He's pretty fucking powerful now. I bet there's no way he'd want that shit leaked." Pausing the feed before it reaches the section where he kills her—because even I have a hard time looking at it—I turn to Death. "Show him what you have."

He pulls his phone out. "You sure? I mean, we talked about this before. This—"

"Yeah. Go," I reply as he hits the play button.

Cap looks confused, but he won't be for long. As the video plays, a feed of Death, Curse, and Destroyer unloading boxes upon boxes of drugs from the back of a banana truck. "You sure you can move this much?"

"Yeah, we can. We have the resources. More than anyone else on the West Coast. We got this," Death states, handing over a case presumably for payment of the shipment he's just received.

"Good. I'd hate to have to kill your whole club over a few kilos." Shaking hands with Death, the video pans out from the side. I've already seen this, so the shock is minimized with me. Not so much with Cap and Raptor.

Standing beside King—who's smiling as wide as a Cheshire—the man in a neatly pressed suit like King grins. "Controlling one club at a time, King."

"One at a time," he replies, clearly pleased with himself. "Did the Bows send you the latest shipment in good order?"

"*Severo*," someone calls out.

"Yeah." He turns toward them.

"Boss, the plane is ready."

"Gotta go, King," the man says without answering the previous comment about us. I know he received it in good order, I heard that True delivered it personally with Nock and two of the other boys. Two that are long since dead after a bad run.

"Back to the mansion on the hill?"

Not answering King, he comments, though we still can't see his face. When it pans up, the man that I know Cap will know immediately on sight comes into view. "You watch my business here or I'll find a way to fucking gut you, King. I have more friends than you have enemies." Turning away, he leaves King on the curb, worried and fearful.

Pausing the feed, Death sets his phone on the table and turns to the group. "Now do you see the urgency? The Alta Noche are taking over our area, one club, one drug buy, one gun run at a time. We're the DEAs pet project in the west. We're the Alta Noche's little mules."

Everyone at the table is quiet as they consider the consequences of the videos they've watched. Rap, Cap, and I are the only ones, though, that get the whole picture. We see who's controlling who.

"Is this the first time you've seen him, Severo or King?" I ask the Heartless Bastards.

"I've only ever had dealings with King. Fucker never sat right with me, but he offered terms and product that suited us." Soulless is steaming inside. The look on his face tells the story. He must have an issue with blood pressure, as his face has deepened to a dark ruby red. He obviously had no idea the guy had connections to the Alta Noche in the way he does. Yeah, he's been crafty in making sure we knew he was DEA, and that with the flick of his fingers he could lock us all away for good, total club and all. Though knowing he was running it all through the Alta Noche, that, it seems, was a surprise.

Looking at Cap, his gaze has softened slightly. "Did King approach you like he has the rest of us?"

Shocked, he blinks a few times before snapping himself out of the internal thoughts about what he's just learned. Our father wasn't in jail like we'd assumed. He's running Alta Noche, and he's been playing all the clubs. He's fucking working with King, and is the king of his own extensive enterprise in Mexico to boot.

As soon as Death showed me this video back at the hospital, I knew we had to fix this.

"Who wants a Soul Shaker?" Oubliette crows as she walks toward the table, teetering eight glasses.

Before I can answer her, Death says, "Thanks, babe. That sounds great." As he's handed one of the highballs, Obi smiles back.

Placing a drink in front of each of us, or handing it to us directly, Obi smiles at me before she wanders away. No muss. No whining she's not involved in the conversation. Nothing. That woman is—

"God, she's somethin' else," Death notes as he sips the florescent green concoction. "Damn. That woman is near perfect. I hope you understand that, Busta."

Took the words right out of my mouth, Death. "Trust me, I'm not missing the mark," I reply, watching her sway away.

Leaning on the table, pulling our attention away from Obi, Rap pushes the drink to the center of the table. "We're going against them how? A little video doesn't do much, guys. Not against the fucking corrupt government agency and a fucking drug lord."

"We'll work out Grim." Looking at Cap, I know it will take both of us in some capacity. "Common enemy. Common goal. For now, we need to close up our ties on this side. We need to use Hart to end our relationship with King, and we'll have to go legit all around. No more 1%. No more dangerous cargo and unsavory goods. Anyone opposed to that?"

"As long as we can continue to make money?" Soulless pipes up. Taking a smell of his glass, he sips it tentatively. "This shit is good."

Gulping down a mouthful, Soulless is content with the drink she supplied. "What the fuck's in there?"

"I never ask. She won't tell ya anyway," Death crows. We both know she's a fucking gem with drink creations, and I don't dare tell him in what other capacities she's well versed in. He and Jazzy have been like family to her, so the last thing he wants to hear is how well she fucks.

Cap resting back in his chair, arms crossed and leveling a deep look of hatred at me still. "So let's work this out then. You seem to be the man with the plan, so tell the rest of the class, *Busta*." His cynicism is expected, and I can't deny that he has every right to be mad at me, but we need to work this out. And fast.

"This is what I was thinking..."

O<u>ubliette</u>

Bringing them the drinks I'd created, I pulled a drop and run. That was after a quick hello to Bennett. The last thing I want is to be in the way, or to break up their power meeting. I was so happy to see Death and Trigger. Even Radish perked up as she heard my voice. That felt good.

As always, I try not to overhear things, but I couldn't help noticing that Lucius and Cap were mirror images of each other. Damn near perfect replicas. The same skin tone, the same build, the same mannerisms, the same defensive stances. Damn near the same eyes—and the only difference I could see was their facial hair. Where Busta has a fantastic beard, Cap has a clean-shaven look. He has a ton of tattoos that peek out under his shirt and cut, and a glaring stare that states death to Lucius. If they were given a chance, I'm not sure I could place bets on the winner.

Checking out the bar, I restocked the shelves and rearranged shit that someone had put back in the wrong spot to keep myself busy. I never wanted to know their business, and I'm trying my hardest not to know now. Keeping away kept me from being a participant. That, unfortunately, hasn't worked.

Shuffling a stack of paperwork, I find a picture of my brother, Grady. "Shit. He's gonna fucking murder me if I don't call him soon." Normally, Grady and I see or speak to each other at least once every couple days. With all of this going on, I've only called to say I was alive and to check in. I haven't, and won't tell him about the murder, the kidnapping, the other murder, and my secondary hostage taking, mainly because he couldn't have done shit about it. My brother is a big guy, and yeah, he works out, but even he wouldn't be a match for any of these guys. Grady is an investment banker down the street, and he's a wet noodle compared to them. Still, he's gotta be pissed I haven't called.

Picking up the bar phone, I walk off to one of the booths. I won't go to the back area by myself again, as I can't make myself relive those memories, and if I walk over, I'll just be an interruption they don't need.

Slinking away from the bar, Lucius tracks my moves with his eyes. Holding up the phone, I point to the booth on the far side. I don't want him worrying about me. Heck, after my *fear* confession of being alone today, I'm amazed Lucius even let me have a moment of peace in the change room. I think I freaked him out. That's only fair, as I've been freaked out and scared. He might as well be a bit too.

Sliding into the booth, I dial Grady. Two rings in and he answers. "Hello? This better be my sister. This is my sister, right? Not some biker telling me she's been shuttled to the moon or some shit."

"Hey, Grady. How are you?"

"How am I? How do you think I am? We haven't spoken in almost two weeks, and that boss of yours—Granite, or whatever, wouldn't tell me what was going on! I even checked your condo. You haven't been there. Know how I know? Your favorite plant is dying. I watered it. You're welcome." His voice reaches prepubescent tones. He's pissed off.

"I'm fine, Grady. Really, I'm okay."

"You don't sound okay. You sound hushed, like you're trying to hide." Man, he's such a worrywart.

"I'm good, I swear. I'm just somewhere that people are having a meeting and I don't wish to interrupt. So, any news?" I ask.

"Usual."

Wow, that was stated too fast. "Grady..."

"Nothing you need to worry about right now, Obi." I know he wasn't feeling well a few weeks back, and he was having tests done, but he's avoiding talking about it. I *know* when he's avoiding. I'll leave it for now, as I have things I don't want to talk about either. Not like I can get into it.

"Grady—"

"I'm glad you're calling. I need to travel for a bit, Obi. Do you think you could watch Kessel?" His voice falters. I can tell something profound is bothering him. With all the shit lately, the last thing I can handle is a lie from my brother. I won't tell *him* the truth, so it's kind of hypocritical.

"Tell me what's going on, Grady. Please."

"Like you've told me?" Taken aback by his harshness, he cuts in before I can reply, "Sorry, Obi. That wasn't fair."

"It's okay, I get it. I haven't been very forthcoming."

"So you'll watch Kes?" he asks again.

"Of course I can watch Kessel. I love that damn dog."

He clears his throat. "Um...Obi, I'm at work and it's month's end. I gotta go."

Feeling a bit choked up, saddened that he's shooing me off the phone, I say, "Grady, I swear I'll see you soon. We'll talk."

With a pause on the line, I know he's thinking of how to get out of the conversation, and how to ask me what's going on at the same time. He avoids it, though. "Love you, Obi."

I smile into the phone. "Love you too, Grady."

Setting the phone on the table after I hang up, I do my best to control the emotions that I've been holding in. The kidnapping, being back here, the memories of the cage and Nock—all of it is weighing on me. Now I'm withholding from Grady and he knows it.

When our parents died in a car crash, Grady looked after me. He made sure we were fed, clothed, housed, and that I went to school like our parents had wanted. I did everything he asked or said, as I feared if I didn't that I'd be alone. That the reason we were alone was because I'd always rebelled. I miss our parents every day, and Grady is all I have left. I tell him everything—except for this. I know I'll have to, just not yet.

Looking over to the men at the table talking in harsh tones, concern laces their features, and I know something profound is going on. I'm glad I'm not a part of it. I've had enough of being a part of anything that has to do with this. I'll stick with creating their drinks and hopefully a little more time with Lucius. Sure, I've seen these guys with girls—revolving doors, a smack on the ass and a 'later, darlin'' as they ddo the walk of shame away. I don't have big plans for us. In all honesty, I have no plans for us. I don't think that far ahead. I still kind of think this is one of those Stockholm Syndrome type hostage things. I fell for the captor because he brought me cookies.

I know he feels remorseful, but I've been around these guys long enough that I know they're not the marrying type. No white picket fences, no two kids that are perfect shining examples of the community, and no husband who with a kiss on the cheek takes off to his acceptable job.

As I'm laughing to myself at the audacity of him in a suit and tie, Lucius' phone vibrates. I watch him. His stance stiffens, and his body hardens as he rises out of the chair fast, while the others start to scramble around. Walking over to my booth, the look on his face is hardened and worried. With that panty-melting smile, I see him trying to hide something.

"What's wrong?" I ask, though I honestly don't expect an answer.

"Things are in motion, faster than we thought. I need you at the clubhouse for your safety. Do you mind if I have Miss swing by your place quick and grab clothes? Fuck, he's really worried.

"Yeah, of course. No problem at all."

Hopping on the bike, we ride off toward the Broken Bows and whatever fate has in store for me.

B<u>usta</u>
Fuck!

No, really. Fuck!

Rushing to the bike, trying not to worry Obi, I text Miss her address as she recites it.

I told him that I'd be fine and didn't need his ass to follow me around like a fucking prick. I didn't need an escort to Humble, and because of our meet, I didn't bring heat. I've left us vulnerable. That means more to me than worrying about myself.

Strapping her helmet on, Obi hops up on the back of the bike without argument. "Hold on, love. We're gonna go a bit fast."

Starting my bike and pulling out of the lot as if the wings of hell are attached, I rush us through the center of town toward the clubhouse. Yellow stop lights were green as far as I was concerned. Nothing was stopping me from getting her to safety.

I tried to be involved fully in our meet, but with her there—after her revelation earlier—I couldn't take my eyes from her for long. Even letting her out of my sights in the back, I was on edge. When I received a text, at first I wasn't going to look at it, but when I saw it flash up with King's name, and a comment that stated *"She's pretty. What are we up to, boys?"* with a picture of us walking into Humble through the sight of a gun, I didn't argue. We moved as fast as we could.

Pulling down the highway to the clubhouse, I watch every car, every person on the street, and every business window or rooftop for threats. I've never felt so afraid to lose someone. Slowing at a red light, I turn down a side street instead of stopping on purpose.

Hugging her arms around me, Oubliette strokes my abs. It's soothing, not erotic in any way. Whoever put this woman in my path, I need to buy them a whiskey and offer my thanks. True. Well, he's six feet under—or thereabout, and he doesn't deserve it.

Knowing the distance, I'm watching every turn and street. Three more lights then she's safely tucked away. Counting down each light, curve and blinker strike, two prospects stand at the gate. Opening it for us, I pass through and park on the right.

Shutting off the bike, I ask her, "Obi, you good?"

Unbuckling the helmet, she shakes out her hair. "I might need a hair tie and some conditioner to straighten it back out, but otherwise, I'm good." Stepping off, I help her down by way of holding those fabulous hips.

Setting her on her feet, I kiss her on the forehead and smile as she strokes my beard. "Go, be dangerous. I'm fine."

Oh how she understands this life and what I intend to do. I can't express how it warms my heart. "I'm sorry, Obi, but I do have to go."

Opening the door, she steps into the darkened room. "I'm good. Really, Busta. Go do what you have to. I'm sure you have more important things to do than to watch over me."

There you're wrong, Oubliette. I avoid that comment, as there's nothing more important that her safety.

Releasing her, she breathes hard as I pull away. "You're mine, Oubliette. As soon as I can, you'll have a property patch on that fabulous ass. Consider yourself an owned woman."

She gives me a cocky grin. "What if I don't want to be owned?"

"No choice in the matter." I lean in and whisper, "I'd chase you to the ends of the earth." Kissing her sweetly again, even as the room erupts in catcalls and whistles, I stroke her hair smooth. "Gotta go now, woman. I'll see you in a bit. Stay safe." Looking around the room, I immediately see Panna. "Hang out with Pan. Keep the old lady out of trouble, okay?"

"Yeah. Okay, Lucius." She smirks before walking off to the bar.

"Miss, Munch, Flight, and Smart. Church." Miss called in everyone before the meet, locking down the club tighter than a virgin ass, and I'm more than happy for it. He was the right guy to be my VP.

"Already on it, boss," Miss answers. Looking around the room, I notice we're minimal right now. There's a lack of membership in the clubhouse. It feels awkward.

"Where is everyone?" I ask him as we're walking down the hall.

"I had to send a few out on a run for food. We were low on groceries after the lockdown. They'll be back any minute."

As he and I pass through the door and close it behind us, I ask the others, "Did Miss let you in on the meet today?"

Nodding their heads, we run it down. While I show them the text from Death and the picture, the consensus is to bring blood to the San Bernardino streets. I know in my heart that King is behind this. Someway, somehow, he's the culprit.

Gathering up all the guns we can muster on the bikes without being conspicuous, we head out the door, leaving instructions with the guys left behind that no one enters but us.

No one.

O ubliette

"Hey, Panna. Up for a few rounds of guess the drink?" I ask her as I approach.

"Hell no. The hangover lasted all day. I'm not sure I can handle restarting so soon." Smiling and walking over to the bar with me, she takes the seat where she sat only hours before. "I heard Busta. Property, huh?"

Yeah, that. "Well, I guess we'll talk about it. I'm sure he's offered it up before. I might have to take the jacket off the last girl first." Grinning like a fool, I walk behind the bar, as Quiver isn't there.

"Last girl?" Giggling in her dark, throaty tone, Panna reaches over the bar, grabbing the wet cloth to wipe it down. "There's never been *a girl*. Never mind a last girl, Oubliette."

"Never?"

Another lady that was sitting at the bar, smacks her hand down and laughs. "No. Never. True thought Busta'd screw his way through the San Bern phone book. Stating property is a huge thing for Busta."

Her perfect, tight, shoulder-length black curls, meticulous make-up and dangling gold hoops create a beautiful lady. I'm jealous. My hair has wonky curls, my blue eyes and soft complexion makes me either burnt or stark white, and my ears are so small, they can't hold a hoop that size. I damn well wish they could. I don't know this lady, she wasn't here when we were drinking before, so I introduce myself as I pour Panna and I a drink I call the Mummy. "I'm Oubliette. And you are?"

"Scarlet." Her voice is soft and saddened as she raps her long fingers on the bar. "True was my guy. The old VP turned pres, now dead." Lifting a neat whiskey to her lips, it's easy to see she's been sitting here a while.

The look from Panna tells me not to go there, but I do. I've never been one to shy away when someone was at my bar.

"I'm sorry. I'm sure he was a good guy." Mixing a few of the liquors I need, I try to engage her.

"He was an asshole's asshole. He was nasty, mean, and downright awful. True was no more than a serial liar, killer, and manipulator." She lifts her drink in a mock toast. "To True. I'm fucking glad you're gone. No more..." She pauses. "Just, no more." Downing the last of her glass, she lays it on the bar top and walks away.

Blinking a few times, completely confused by the interaction, I finish making mine and Panna's second drinks. The first won't last long. Sliding it across to her, I ignore the oversized crazy camel in the room. That doesn't stop Panna, though.

"Sorry. She's a box of chocolates you don't normally want to open. She's a bit messy. DG, True's dad and the old president, had messed with her family, her, and her mind for years. She wasn't an old lady, but she was True's girl through and through. He wouldn't admit to it, but she was loyal as fuck and so was he. It was DG that wouldn't let him mark her as property, so she's important, but not a protected member like being property would be."

"Got it." I think.

Shrugging her shoulders, she continues. "She's not normally a wreck. Scarlet is usually the first to be sober in a crisis."

"I haven't wanted to be the sober one in a crisis, so I envy her."

Leaning across the bar, moving closer to me, Panna whispers, "Can I tell you something?"

"Bartender," I state, like it's a reason to trust me implicitly.

"She's been gone for a few days. Missing. I heard one of the guys say she'd been walked out of a police station by DEA agents, but it's hearsay. I don't put much in hearsay." Leaning back again, she grins mischievously. "Now pillow talk. That I trust fully." With a wink, she upends her drink to her mouth.

Hell, I'm so happy I met this woman. I understand how Lucius says she's his favorite.

For the next hour, Panna, myself, and a few other old ladies gather around. We swig, swill, pour, pout, laugh and joke about life. It feels fantastic. The guys are still in their meeting, or those that were stationed to protect us and the families. They're on high alert, and they stay *far* away from the bar. They leave us to our wicked devices, stating it's not safe near me and my concoction brewing when they need their wits about them.

Finally relenting when my bladder can't handle more, after too many drinks and not enough breaks, I wander off to the bathroom. The last time here I was confronted. This time is no different.

Opening the door, I almost slam straight into Scarlet. "Shit. Sorry, Scarlet," I say, nearly plowing her into the sink.

"No harm," Scarlet replies as she turns to the mirror.

Closing the stall door behind me, getting about my business as fast as I can, the rush feels almost orgasmic. Not like Lucius orgasmic, 'cause that's fucking epic, but more like a moment alone in my own home kind. Finishing up after what feels like at least ten minutes, I walk out to wash up. Scarlet's still here, leaning on the sink and looking at me. This is starting to be the weirdest meeting place ever.

With a sweet smile, I ask her, "Could you pop to the side for a second, Scarlet? I'd like to wash up."

She comes out of her trance. "Yeah. Sorry." She steps to the side.

Turning on the water, rinsing my hands and drying them on the towel, Scarlet hasn't moved. It's unnerving, but like Panna said, she's a bit messed up from the previous administration.

"You know, I've been here a long time."

Oh shit.

"And in that time, I've done what was best for my own survival. If I was told to do something, I did it. No questions, no balking at the request. I just did it."

This bathroom is starting to be my *least* favorite room. Even though the cell at the warehouse was a front-runner for the worst in my history, this bathroom is now making its way up to the head of the pack.

"I'm being asked again to do something. I'll apologize to you now, though." Lifting a pistol, the silvery shine of it pointed my way, Scarlet has me fearing where this is going.

Hoping I can talk her down, I try diplomacy. "Scarlet, I don't know what this is about, but I'm sure there's a better way out of it than to kill me."

"I'm not about to kill you. No. That's not my job." Lifting a phone, she hits a button and a call connects on speakerphone.

"Yeah," the voice crows over the tiny speaker.

"I have the woman you asked for." I don't even merit a name. Well, that sucks.

"Meet us at the side door toward the residence. I'm outside." As he hangs up, she pockets the phone.

"Time to go, Oubliette." Swinging the gun my way, she indicates that I'm to go out ahead of her.

Can I walk out and hit the front area without a bullet for the attempt? Probably not. But also, if the person waiting is somehow working against Busta, I have to find out who and stop them before they ruin his club—or worse, kill him.

He's a good guy. It's been a short time, but I've grown attached to the growly hunk. That means my intrepid intrigue is piqued. I want to know who it is.

Praying that one of the burly guys will come down the hall toward us, saving me from the decision, I step out of the bathroom.

"Whoa, sorry. I almost knocked you over." Panna smiles as she grasps my shirt before falling backward.

"It's okay, Panna. No harm." I hope my wide-eyed look attracts her attention, saving me from the fate of whoever the bachelor is behind door number two.

"You better, Scarlet?" Panna asks with true interest.

Looking over my shoulder at Scarlet, I watch in slow motion as a bystander.

"Sorry I have to do this, but I never liked you Pandora." Letting off a shot, there's no sound in the tight corridor, and the shocked look on Panna's face is just as insane as mine. Collapsing to the floor, I try to catch Panna on the way, attempting to break her fall.

"Oh my God!" I yell out as I watch blood leech out of a wound in her waist.

"Why?" Panna implores.

With a stern gaze, Scarlet pushes the gun to my head. "There's no other way."

Chapter

O<u>ubliette</u>

If I thought that seeing Nock die by my hand was bad, it was nothing compared to this. Holding my hands on the open wound, I desperately want to cry out for help. I can't, though, not with the muzzle end of the gun on my head and the threat of *'not a word'* spoken by Scarlet.

"Stand up. It's time to go." She pushes the gun into my scalp. She must have a silencer on it because I don't remember hearing a noise, and no one ran down the hall to the sound of a gunshot.

"Panna—" I start, but Scarlet interjects.

"She can yell out for help once we're gone. Now up ya get. It's time for your grand exit."

"Are you fucking kidding me?" Come on, universe. I've had enough of this.

Hitting me on the head, not so gently, Scarlet spews her sour words. "Yeah, I'm not one for kidding. Let's go."

I shift Panna's hands to cover the wound where my hands move from. "Panna, make sure you keep pressure here. Call out for Ret—"

"Come on," Scarlet impatiently calls out. "We don't have time for this."

Looking up at her, I'm pissed. Truth of it right there. I'm seething mad that she'd let Panna die. How nasty is this lady, and how badly does she want me alive? If I rebel, will she kill me? Will she let me go?

"She'll die. Let me help her at least before—"

Turning the gun, she points it at Panna and shoots again. "There. No reason for you to worry about her. Let's go, Oubliette. I don't have time for this."

Pulling my hair, yanking me off the floor, Scarlet directs me away. The whole time, I don't dare take my eyes from Panna. I won't let her die alone. Wrestling against Scarlet, I try desperately to stay. I pull down as she pulls up even harder. I feel the hair tearing and ripping, but it's a small price to pay.

"Fuck off!" Swinging wildly with my arms backward, hoping to hit any part of her that throws her off, I fight.

"You don't get it. You don't get a choice." Kicking me in the back of the knees, I fall over, but she pulls desperately on my hair, dragging me down the hall. I fight as hard as I can, that is, until I hear the wheeze of death from Panna. I never thought it would be a sound I could distinguish from another, but hearing it with Nock, it's now a dark friend.

With the gun at my head, she pulls at my hair. "Get up, Oubliette. Or I'll wait for another club member to come down this hall and I'll slug another bullet in someone. Your choice. Pandora only, or another dies too? Tick tock, Oubliette. Tick tock."

Pausing my fight, taking one last look at Panna and her deadened eyes, I rise off the floor. Standing toe-to-toe with Scarlet, I glare at her. Her eyes are cool, unfazed by the murder she's committed, and uncaring that she's quite content to cause further destruction.

"Move," is all she says, motioning for me to walk down the hall to the outer door.

The door itself is solid, no light filtering through and no windows. Whoever is on the other side is a mystery. I can't believe I'm in a dangerous situation again. I imagine being anywhere but here. Anywhere but here with her would be fine. I'd pay to be put back in that warehouse. At least I know I left a weapon. I'd have something to use against her.

Changing tactics, using her psychosis of 'I'm doing what's best,' I appeal to her. "I hope this is worth it to you. I hope giving up everything and everyone is worth it. You won't have anywhere to turn that the Bows won't find you." I'm doing anything I can to appeal to her final thread of decency. I doubt there's more than that single thread, since she's dark and disgusting inside. She left Panna on the floor like trash and wouldn't let me help save her.

She doesn't answer.

Fuck, I need to escape.

Walking to the door, I think of all the opportunities I have left to get away or to call out for help. Man, I always thought that clubs were full of men—strong, armed, dangerous and cunning. Not the case.

This woman has entered the den of the dangerous and upped the game. After what Lucius told me of the Madox men, I don't think she's as much a victim as a full participant.

Passing a few doors, one that is marked laundry, another supplies, nothing stands out that would help. Touching the handles, trying them to see if I can at least hide out, Scarlet smacks my hand with the gun. "Stop that. I already locked all the doors beforehand. Like I'd be stupid enough to give you an out." Pushing the muzzle of the gun into the small of my back, against my spine, I grimace and walk on.

Approaching the door, I think of only one other way out of this—push through and run like hell. Preparing mentally for the escape, setting my hand on the slam bar to pop the door, I turn and ask, "You know they'll hunt you down. You know Lucius won't stop. I hope whoever offered you this great prize had an understanding of what you'd give up to get it."

Placing the barrel on my neck, reaching around and pushing the door, she says, "What I got in return was more than worth it."

Oubliette

With the light of day blinding me, I step out unwillingly. Temporarily blinded, I move toward the sunshine. Mainly as I don't have another choice.

"Well, well. I didn't think you'd make it out here. I had bets on you, Scarlet." Blinking to clear the light away, I'm shoved forward.

"I said I could do it, sir. I knew I could. You need better trust in my abilities." With the door closing behind us, Scarlet shoves me hard into the arms of the man outside.

"So lovely to be introduced properly, Oubliette. You've caused me a lot of heartache and paperwork, young lady." That irks me more than this hostage taking. The last person to call me young lady was my mother, pissed off at me for a dirty bedroom. She's been dead for quite a while. The words carry a different meaning for me. It reminds me that I need to be the best I am, to show my parents that I could be better than that rotten teenager. That I can excel and be amazing at everything I do. This asshole calling me a young lady makes my blood boil.

Now that my eyes have adjusted to the stark difference, I take in the man before me. It's the prick at Lucius' house the other day. King, Lucius called him.

"Sorry to rush you away from your adoring fans, but we have somewhere to be." He smiles at me, making my skin crawl. I'd rather a box full of scorpions running across my body than to be anywhere near this man. His whole demeanor and attire is skeezy. He's not afraid to lie, cheat, steal, destroy, and start the cycle back over to get what he wants. Him, I'm afraid of.

Looking around the area behind him, I search for something, anything that can save me. I'm disappointed that the nearest building is a good twenty feet away. The men are still in their meeting and they'd never hear me from here, so I change tactics. Bravado it is.

I cross my arms and plant my feet. "What do you want with me? I'm no one special."

"Au contraire, my friend. You are so special. It's beautiful how much you're needed." He turns to Scarlet. "You're needed more than *her*, Oubliette."

What?

I don't get it. I might be kind of missing something here, but she called him sir, so I have the feeling she works for him. So how does that make me more important?

"I don't believe you. Why would I be?" I finally ask.

"Lucius. He's my end game," he answers nonchalantly, and without inflection. Pulling a pistol from his waist, he aims at Scarlet. "You're replaceable."

Piping up, sounding stressed, Scarlet pulls me toward her. "You promised me, Magnus. My parents—"

Firing a shot, I don't dare look. I honestly don't need to. Releasing her hold on me, feeling wetness coating me, and the thunk noise of a body hitting the ground, that tells me all I need to know. Scarlet's dead.

Another on account of me. Everyone is falling like the pieces on a chessboard. Each player that thought they were important are finding they were a lowly *pawn*. They can't take down the queen. None have the strength. In this case, King, the knight, is still holding the power, holding the queen at bay. It's a losing battle.

"Now." Holstering his gun with a flat expression, he tosses something to the ground. Taking a peek at it, it falls open at my feet with her picture and a badge that shines proudly. DEA. "How about we get this show on the road without further bloodshed. I assume you'd approve of that, right, Oubliette?" Spinning on his expensive shiny brown loafers, King extends an arm, asking for me to go first. In a daze, I start in the direction requested.

Slipping around the side of the low brick building, we arrive at the front where I've entered a few times. The area is packed full of bikes, with the majority of the guys in their 'church.' I'm alone. There are a few cars, of which I assume are the ladies', but no one loitering around.

There's a truck and three men whom are suited identically beside darkened SUVs. DEA courses their vests. Their tactical. Each of them adorned in clothing that you'd assume of their position. With guns drawn, stark, unfeeling stares, and three Broken Bows members on their knees before them, the officers hold all the power. One of them is the prospect I drank with last night. Two are men that I hadn't met yet but had seen around. Again, prospect is plastered against the rocker on their cuts. With their hands crossed on their heads, they're at a serious disadvantage to the military precision of the heavily armed agents.

"We're ready, sir. Where's Scarlet?" One of the agents speaks up, standing over the prospect.

"She won't be joining us. She reached the end of her usefulness."

"Fuckin' pigs," One of the prospects, Sinew, mutters darkly before the agent smacks him across the head with the butt of the gun, knocking him unconscious.

Looking at the passed-out body, the agent sneers. "Shut the fuck up. You're just another robot towing the company line." He mocks him, "*We're bad assholes.* It's bullshit, kid. You haven't done enough wrong in your life to earn that attitude. You can't even grow a beard yet. Pussy." Laughing, he and his agent buddies smile and laugh at the ribbing that the poor unconscious Sinew takes.

"Okay, let's go, boys. Oubliette, after you, my dear." King motions, directing me to an awaiting blacked-out SUV.

Popping the door, King gives me no choice. I've seen Scarlet and his resolve to show me how dangerous he can be. How deep his disregard for life runs. I always thought the government, the police, and people of power were held to higher standards. That life was precious.

Not so.

Sliding across the seat, I move to exit out the other side, as King isn't quite in yet. Reaching the far seat, the door pops. The agent that clocked Sinew climbs in. Staying in the middle, another man climbs in on the other side.

Peeking his head within, King chirps, "You know where to go. We have a date that we're late for as it is. He never likes being made to wait, Johnson."

The man behind the wheel shifts the truck into gear with a decisive "Yes, sir."

Pulling out of the Broken Bows compound, I look back. Lying on the ground is Sinew and the other men. I'm stuck once more where I don't wish to be.

I'm squeezed between two large men with guns.

This grand adventure to hell and back is becoming increasingly worse.

Chapter

B<u>usta</u>
"Here's the evidence. What do you mean you can't do anything?" I'm fucking pissed. This was our last chance to sideline King legally.

Leaving the clubhouse in a rush, taking all of our evidence with us, we kept going with the plan. My head and heart weren't in it, but neither was Death's. Thing is, we knew this had to be done. Leaving our families behind, those we cared about most. We knew that this had to be addressed with Johnathan Hart.

Shrugging snuggly behind his desk, Johnathan Hart isn't as afraid as I wanted him to be. I wanted him to see that Magnus King had been dealing both sides of the law, that he'd been playing dirty all along. I was no one's pawn, but I had been playing a part in his match nonetheless, and I'd had enough of it. I wanted out of the game.

"Lucius, I get it. You and I have a history. I understand your predicament with the law, but King is, and always has been, the legal means to us closing down the clubs on the West Coast. You were brought in for that means. You were to infiltrate, report, and decisively crush the illegal trades in this little part of our world."

I'm really wishing I'd brought my piece with me now. I'd love nothing better than to put a bullet through his smug face and gladly see it lodged into the cheap wood paneling behind him.

I came in here with Death, and his look reflects mine. The two of us were handing over the evidence we had on King to Hart, to bring King down for good. To shut down his destructiveness. Hart, as the head of the Homeland division, sees King as a tool that's necessary. He's a dark need in a dark world.

Here's the thing about that: I expected the answers we're being given. Death did too. We didn't expect to have our request allowed, assisted, or even given authority. That's fine by me. That just means I do this my way. The Bow way.

Rising off the wall I'd been leaning on, I step up to the desk. Johnathan seems sort of fearful as I approach, and he should be. I don't need a gun to harm him. I'm scarier without one. I've never had a problem with calling bullshit and doling out pain to those that deserve it. He knows that better than most.

Realizing early on in the conversation that we weren't going to get anywhere, I act as if I'm pissed, but resigning myself to the fact that I can't do a thing. I'll play my part if need be. No worries about that, Hart. I've become a fantastic actor, master at manipulation, and a king of bullshit.

Talking in a lower tone, seeming annoyed but understanding of his position, I reply, "That's fine. I get it, Hart. I do. You're a paper pusher. You can't do anything about it because he's doing what he was created for. He's cleaning house and making you look like the good guys." Looking over at Death, he has the same look. The one that says we've done what we set out to do. "Ready to go?"

I start across the room. "Yeah, I've had enough bureaucracy for one day. I'd like to go before it rubs off on my cut. I'd have to burn it to remove the awful fuckin' stench." Grasping the door handle, Death leaves within seconds.

As I turn and walk away, Hart calls out, "My hands are tied, Lucius." He's only doing it to make himself feel better. Not to show he's helpful or anything like that. Cunt.

Turning heel, starting for the door, I'm glad. I did what I said I would. I tried to go the way of the law first. I'm still technically on the payroll—that's what Hart reminded me, and King hinted to—so I had to use that to my advantage. 'Use the tools in your bag,' Dad always said. Even a blunt instrument can be dangerous.

I may not be blunt, but I'm sure as shit ready to work with all the opportunities afforded me. As a Bow. As a DEA. As a man that knows how to cause mayhem and get what he wants when he wants it.

Stepping into the hall as we start across the desk-ridden room, joining Death, his phone rings in his pocket. Pulling it free, looking at the number as we walk to the elevator bank, his face screws up. He has no idea who it is.

He raises it to his ear. "Who's this?"

"What do you want?" Pausing, listening to the other end, his attitude changes. The calm man has been replaced with a pissed off whirling dervish. Swinging his arms, looking for something to hit, his face is the epitome of seething mad. "She better not be harmed. I'll fuck up your shit so that even a coroner can't decipher if you're a man or a woman!"

The room stills as Death freaks out. Every face turns our way, and slowly tries to shift back from the dangerous biker who's losing his shit.

Only one man can have that effect on anyone—King.

Turning my way, looking over with strained anger, he hands me the phone. "I can't..." He walks off to punch the nearest wall over and over. As he slams his hands into the sheetrock, I take the phone.

"Hello, Lucius." Fucking King.

"What in the Christ do you want, King?"

"Is that any way to treat a friend who's taking care of something you love? Say hello, Oubliette."

No. This can't be happening. This is beyond words.

Not again. Not her.

"Oh, you're speechless, Lucius. I didn't think that could happen, but color me impressed." Pausing for dramatics, he laughs before continuing. "I'll bet your friend Bennett is having a bit of a fit right now. That might be my fault. His sister is out of his reach. So is Oubliette." His tone is condescending and smug. "You know, you two really should keep a better eye on your toys."

Still slamming his fist into the wall, the blood stains the edges where he's wrecked his hands. I have a need to do the same, to pummel something or someone. Someone named King would feel the best right now, that's for sure.

"What do you want, King?" I ask, trying to keep my voice even.

"Well, I'm so glad you asked. I'd like you to meet me and a mutual friend at the warehouse that you recently closed up. You can bring your brother and his club too, but only two men from each club, max. We wouldn't want a war with such delectable women in the area. Stray bullets can cause issues.

"What do you say...an hour from now? That should give you a moment or two to gather your troops. Oh, and remember, Lucius, I have more men at my disposal than you do. Plus, they have no issue with taking out pieces of shit for the fun of it. So be good and stick to the rules. See you there." With the dial tone appearing in my ear, I finally set the phone on the table before me. The need to tear something down is a driving force.

Waiting for Death to wear himself out from destroying the wall, I gather every ounce of hatred I have for King and store it up. I'll need every piece of it to take him down. If I take his friends with me on the way, I don't care.

"He has Jazzy and Oubliette. He knew." He slams his fist into the wall again. "He *knew!* He wanted us to team up. He expected it. Fucker wants me so pissed off I'll tear his balls off and feed them to the pigeons."

Standing by as he pulls himself together, I tell him the only thing that makes sense. "He has no idea what he's asking for. We're going to rain down hell."

Turning to me with a darkness in his eyes, he looks the part of a dangerous predator. "I won't care who's in my way. I'm saving my sisters."

"No one will harm them. That's a promise."

Chapter

Oubliette

Driving toward the wharf, the warehouse coming into view, my stomach churns and the bile rises to meet my strained fears. What if they haven't been here and cleaned up the mess from Nock? What if there are no weapon for me to defend myself with? What if they place me in a cell far away...

Too many variables, and I'm fucking freaking out. King knows this is where I was because Lucius explained that it was his connection to the DEA that had me 'freed' in the first place. It was, of course, a setup to keep his association with King kept a secret from the Bows, but he's explained that Bennett is in the same predicament as he is. They've been controlled from the day that King stepped foot in their lives.

What I don't get is what King wants and why he needs me? Why I'm being used at all, and why he killed Scarlet after she'd done as he'd asked?

Asshole with a god complex probably thought he could do anything, that he was untouchable—that rules don't apply to him. Just like True was with Crystal, maniacal and malicious. They have no concept of wrong and right. No concept of the lines they cross to get what they want. Master manipulators.

Christ! Lucius probably doesn't even know I'm gone. If he knows, I'll bet he's losing his shit. He left me in the care of his club when he went out to meet with Bennett. I have no way to tell him what's gone on. King and his agents are in the other truck ahead, and I'm securely surrounded by well-armed men. Knowing a guy like him, he's probably already given Lucius a call and told him I'm in his care. Bullshit. Care is concern. This guy cares for nothing and no one. That's easy to see. He's an egotistical narcissistic asshole.

Turning the corner to the front door of the last place I'd like to visit ever again, King's vehicle stops beside another pair of limo-style SUVs.

Parking beside them and popping the door, the guy to my right steps out. As he stands holding the door, waiting for me to exit. I tentatively shift across the heated leather he'd just occupied. Stepping out into the light, I look to the SUV that held King, just as its doors open and a woman's voice is heard.

"You fucked up, you son of a bitch! I can't wait until my brother skull fucks the remnants of your cracked cranium. I'll gladly boil off the skin and leave you as a lamp on my desk for all eternity!"

Knowing that Jazzy is here both frightens and gives me relief at the same time. "Jaz!" I yell out, moving across the lot to her. Before I can reach her, the first brute to exit our caravan grabs my shirt and hauls me back toward his chest.

"You're staying with me," he says in an awkward tone. His voice is raspy and thick.

Wrestling my shirt out of his grasp, I stand still. I have no issue being defiant, but it'll be stupid to do it now. I need to wait until it's to mine and Jazzy's advantage. We know what's in that warehouse, and if we're lucky, we have ammo. If not, we'll be patient until the rules change and we have an opportunity to free ourselves. Weeks ago, I wasn't as sure of my own survival, but after everything that's happened, I'm willing to go on a little faith. Faith that I can survive this too.

Her eyes twinkle with mischief. They're telling me exactly what I was thinking. *Wait. We'll figure it out.*

Holding still where I am, I wait for permission to start this pantomime of death.

I don't presume that King will allow us to live. We're only here as pawns in his master scheme against Bennett and Lucius. I'm sure King has planned this for quite a time. I doubt it was me directly that was in his plan, but he'd need leverage. At some point, a woman in his life would be leveraged against him. Like Panna said, Lucius hasn't had someone that he's cared for, no one that was old lady material.

Poor Panna. Laid out on the floor of the clubhouse, her life ended for no reason other than gaining me. I still can't understand it. As I look down at my hands, still crusted over, my cuticles are filled with Panna's blood as I tried to save her. Not to mention, the blood splattered along my body from Scarlet. I quickly turn my eyes back up and away from the reminders. Reminders that death has followed me everywhere.

Giving me a shove, the agent tells me to start moving toward the building. Taking steps larger than I normally would, I attempt to catch up to Jasmine. She looks as worn-out as I do, and her body has the same signs of death attached to it. Coming close to reaching out, I grab for her hand. Clasping mine, I feel a sense of relief.

"So glad we can reunite you two," King states with a wide grin. I ignore his barb, and so does Jazzy. We know better than to fight a losing battle. We're outgunned and outmanned, and we know that the interior of the building is so secure, we have no way to escape.

As I look around, hoping for a chance to run like we did before, my personal bodyguard pipes up in a scoffing way, "No use in looking for an escape route. There's no way out." Condescending jackass. Doesn't he see we're grasping at straws and using the only thing we have left? Hope.

"Fucker," I mouth under my breath as he shoves me.

Stepping up to the door, hesitant to enter, I step over the lintel. It looks just like it had when I left—minus the body in the cage. The floor of the cell I occupied has a stain that reflects that of a Rorschach blotter test. Fanned out to the side like devil's wings, the darkest part outlines where Nock lied. His body still burned into my retinas is laid out perfectly in that space. The wings are a manifest as someone attempted to rub the blood remnants away. Hating that I'm here, hating that I have no choice once more, Jasmine and I don't dare release each other's hands. I won't be set in a cell away from her, and I won't be kept alone. I can't. I'll break a little inside as time ticks down the seconds if I'm put back in that same space by myself.

Grasping her hand as if it's the last lifeline, King opens the door. "After you, ladies." He says it with such a sweet tone, that it's as if he's gesturing like a gentleman would at dinner to take the offered seat.

Stepping in and hearing the click of the door as it locks, I turn to face him. I won't give him the power. I won't let him know how much this nine by nine affects me.

Standing outside the door of our cell, King grins. "If you need room service, just ring the bell."

"We'll make sure to call if the pillows are too hard. Or if we wish to cut your balls off and feed them to you." Jazzy smiles in that dark way that only she can. Her dark eyes drilling into his soul as she tells him how she wishes to break and destroy his manhood.

Not answering her, he winks. Staring at me, I give him a look that drills into him the seething contempt that I feel. He smiles before turning toward the stairs.

As each of the agents clomp up the steel stairs, rattling the metal on the way behind him, their receding forms are a blessing. With them leaving us alone, it'll give Jazzy and I time to talk.

With little or no care, Jazzy screams up at his retreating form. "They'll come for us!"

Moving up the steps, seemingly unaffected by her barb, King finally stops on the third. Calling over his shoulder, the silence of the room carries his voice. "Don't worry. We have plans for *the brotherhood*. There'll be no clubs left in the L.A. area when I'm done." Continuing on, decidedly smugger than he had been a moment ago, King finishes walking away from us, and up to the mezzanine.

Once we're fully alone, I turn. Wrapping Jazzy up in my arms as tightly as I can, she reciprocates the squeezing tight hug. "Oh my God! I was so worried about you. I was a total pain to him the whole way here. After we pulled up at the Bows and he walked away...I was so afraid. I heard that gunshot and thought the worst. Seeing you coming around the side I could finally breathe. I was so afraid, sweetie. So afraid."

Breaking the embrace, I wipe the tears away that are spilling down my cheeks, then smile. "Until you stepped out of the car, I thought I was going through this alone. I hate that you're here, but I'm so glad I'm not alone. If I was here with anyone else, I think I'd break apart."

Inspecting our surroundings, I avoid direct eye contact with that smudge on the pavement. I avoid the reminder of my discretionary kill. I search for the glass shard. I hope that they didn't clear it away when they took Nock.

Peering at the base of the cage's edge, I finally see it. I'll leave it in its perfect hiding place and ignore its existence until such time that it's necessary.

"Come on. I think we're stuck in this trap for a bit."

Glancing up at the men in the mezzanine, they've settled in on the couches, grabbed alcohol, and or are taking a snooze. We'll be here a while.

Picking a spot on the floor, away from the marks, and leaving me to look in the opposite direction of the men upstairs, Jazzy and I settle in. "What happened to you? The last I'd heard from Bennett, you were with Busta. I didn't think an asshole like him would let a woman of his out of his sights."

"I'm not his—"

She giggles. "Oh, hun, you're his. I heard from Bennett how our release was planned by him. He told me the whole thing about the pig asshole upstairs that's orchestrated the two clubs, and how protective Lucius has been over you."

I'm taken aback. "He hasn't been protecting me. I mean, we've been at the club and I didn't go home, but that's what Bennett said to—"

Now she's laughing out loud. "Bennett didn't give him directives. Do you honestly think that Bennett is that great at persuasion that he could control the pres of another club? A rival club? Honey, sometimes

I think you're so smart in the ways of flirting and sexual power, then you show me you're so naive about guys."

Smacking her arm, I mock pout. "Not funny, Jasmine. Not funny."

"I'm just ribbing you. I find it funny, though, that you don't see it. That man is so into you, Obi."

The past few hours, with the deaths, and the new hostage/ containment, is totally taking its toll on me. It's cost me energy, emotional and physical strength to fight anything further. Not to mention, the alcohol that was keeping the edge off has worn away. "Jasmine, I'm glad you're here."

"Not sure how I should take that, sweetie."

"In the best way," I reply, yawning.

Cuddling closer, Jasmine wraps an arm around me. "You look worn-out. Take a nap. I'll wake you if something happens."

"I'm not tired."

"And I'm not Ojibway," she huffs sarcastically. "Sleep. Trust me, I got ya."

I close my eyes.

Chapter

B *usta*

When we'd pulled up to the club gate, I immediately knew something was up. Sinew was laid out on the ground. Miss had arrived only moments before me, and he ran inside to check on the rest of the club as I checked on the boys in the yard. The newest prospect, Slam, and his twin brother, Fletch, were checking on Sinew. His clock had been cleaned by one of the DEA agents, as had theirs, but he was still unconscious. Explaining what had happened to a T, they'd confirmed it was King that had dragged away an unwilling Oubliette. None of that was news to me.

When Miss walked out of the clubhouse, I was slightly confused as to why he seemed so sorrowful. I thought the worst. I thought that King had harmed others.

"I know who the mole is."

"Yeah? That's the least of our problems right now I think."

"Not so sure, Pres. Come with me."

As he walked off toward the side of the compound, I muttered to his back, "We don't have time for this shit, Miss."

"You don't have a choice."

Stepping in time behind him, approaching the residence area, I was becoming increasingly annoyed with the delay. We should've been on the road to get Obi.

"Fuck. Whatever it is, we can—" Pausing at the edge of the building, I see the long curly hair of Scarlet fanned out with blood seeping into the stone and dirt path. "Jesus fucking Christ! Are you telling me the mole killed Scarlet? Or she was it?"

Hanging his head, he looks down at a wallet. "She was it." He points to the door. "Inside, you'll find Pandora dead in the hall. Ret isn't taking it well. He only arrived just before us. It looks like Scarlet killed her and took Oubliette. I don't think Scar was ours, I think she was King's." Lifting a discarded DEA badge off the ground, it shows Scarlet's picture and her credentials.

How many people did he have in his control? A better question is, why did he have his fingers in so many pots? Actually, that's simple. He's been making his money off the backs of illegal dealings for years. That's why Hart wouldn't close him down. He must have his hands in the same pot. To take down their informants, it would shut down their incoming cashflow. I'm glad we're stopping it here. This will be the end of it.

Pulling up to the warehouse in under an hour since the call from King, Death and I devised a plan of attack—the rescue. And if things go wrong, how to make sure the girls are protected when it's all said and done. Even if we don't come out of it unscathed, they will.

I contacted both my brother and Soulless and gave them the rundown. Neither of them cared about our girls, but they understood the dangers of letting a cocksucker like King near club property. We were being made an example of, and no one would stand for it.

"You ready?" I ask Death, who's watching the blood from his beaten knuckles continue to drip on the ground beside my truck. We knew taking the bikes would make it harder for a quick escape with the girls, and it would leave them as a target at our backs. In the truck, at least, they could stay out of sight. I grabbed it when we went to the clubhouse to meet up with Miss and Trigger.

I felt bad leaving Radish behind, but with the girls hopping in the vehicle, and the other two guys on bikes, we had nowhere to put the dog that I was comfortable with. Not in a grab and run situation. I know Trigger was a bit annoyed, but in the end, he was more worried about Radish's safety.

Parking down the street from our old warehouse, with Miss resting against his bike, we waited for my brother, Rap, Soulless and Sinner. We'd come prepared with enough firepower to leave King looking like

Swiss cheese, and I know, as do the rest, there's no way King is coming out of this outside of a body bag. His end is here.

Walking over to Miss, he clasps my arm and asks, "Ready?" I know his thoughts are running murderous and rampant like mine. He knows that if it was any woman he loved that was locked in there, I'd do the same for him. Also, I think he fell for Obi and her drink mixing abilities.

As we stand at the corner of wharf two, looking at the front entrance of our old warehouse, I take in the six well-armed DEA agents. With at least two pistols each and an automatic rifle over their shoulders, King has them ready to kill us. I'm not afraid of the odds, we have more to lose and a greater reward.

As a blacked-out pickup rides around the corner, I watch Cap arrive. Pulling up beside my truck after shutting it off, he steps out.

"Here. A little gift," Cap states with a wide grin. Tossing a pinned grenade my way, and holding his own tightly, he shows me he's carrying a block of C-4 too. "I figure I've held onto these long enough. They should be fun."

Smiling and scoffing at his insanity—a craziness that I've missed—I fiddle with the explosive. "This may not be as fun as it is deadly," I laugh, "but I like where your mind's going."

Turning to Rap, I give him a head nod. He's still standoffish, and I can't deny it's well placed. The day I was taken from the Cruel Intentions, it looked as if I had been the cause of the club closing. It's hard to let old wounds heal when they run deep.

"Ready to cause some shit?" I ask.

He repliescoolly, "Yep. This is as good a time as any I guess."

Checking out how Rap is kitted up, I'm glad for the extra assistance. With two fully automatic AKs and a military AR, he's well-appointed.

"We're just waiting on Sinner and Soulless to show, then we'll make our move."

"Sounds fun. I'm gonna hang over here and check out chicks on dating sites," Rap chuckles. Watching him walk off, I place the loaded grenade on the hood of the truck. Situating it so it won't roll off, I check my own gear. I'm carrying two Sig Sauers, a Glock, and pockets full of ammo. I won't take chances. The agents came prepared to put my ass in the dirt, and I'll conveniently do the same.

"You sure she's worth it?" Cap asks in a bored tone.

"Yeah. She's more than perfect, man."

Wincing, nibbling on his lower lip and biting his tongue, I know my brother well enough. He's biting back a rebuttal. He has something to say.

"Spill. What is it that's bugging you, Cody?"

I know that using his real name piques his interest more. It pisses him off too, but I'm going for either at the moment. He's got something to say and I won't go into a fucking war with his head not in the game.

Blowing out a breath, he weighs whether what he wants to say will piss me off, but he relents. "I guess I never thought I'd see you with a little white girl."

Punching him hard across the cheek, his eyes harden and his look is murderous. I'm beyond pissed, though. "Cody, if our mother ever heard you say that, she'd whip your ass then hand you to dad for a good beating." Ready to hit him again, I feel my blood boil for the attitude he's showing. It's King's fault, not Cody's that he even thought to say that aloud. It's King's fault that I wasn't there, that our parents weren't there as he was growing up, and that someone else had a hand in the man he became.

"You're lucky I have someone else to kill or I'd lay you out for that. Until you know Oubliette, you best keep your blatant disrespect to yourself. I've never known you to be that guy, so I hope you just had a lapse in judgement."

Watching as the fire dies out in Cody's eyes, a sorrowful glare replaces it. "Sorry. That was a shit thing to say. I guess I don't really know you anymore, Lu. I don't know shit about her either, so yeah, I'm an asshole." He holds out a hand.

Agreeing, I shake the offered hand. "Yeah, you're right. You're an asshole. But you say shit like that again and I'll knock your fucking teeth out, kid. Pres or no Pres. I won't take that at all. Fair?"

"Yeah, man. Fair." Smiling in that soft cocky way he does, Cody picks up the grenade I left on the hood of his truck. "What are we waiting on?" He looks at his watch. "I thought we only had an hour?"

"You ever thought to be punctual on someone else's time before, brother?"

"Nah, never."

"Good," I say. "Then we'll make him wait a touch longer. I'd rather him antsy and annoyed we're not on time. It'll throw him off."

"What about—" Rap starts, just as Soulless and Sinner in their lowrider car comes around the corner. "Never mind. They're here."

Decked out in purple, the eighties Cadillac rides toward us. With heavy beats thumping it down the alley, the engine and the music stops as a lull goes over our group. We look around at each other, dumbfounded that a seventies ballad was playing in a car owned by one of the most notorious bikers in L.A.

"Hey." Popping the door, Soulless rises to his full height. He's not far off of my brother's size and stature, but what he misses in size, he makes up for in blatant attitude. Over the years, I've had a few run-ins with him. We've become amicable. Soulless takes no shit. He doles out punishment, and if he thinks you've crossed him, you best keep everything you love protected. He'll use every dirty move you can assume, and even those you can't. This is one of those times I'm glad he's sided with us.

Armed to the teeth with knives, and not one gun, I smile. "Close quarters, huh?"

He smirks. "Only way to kill is seeing death scramble across their eyes on the way out."

I can't say I blame him. I agree. When Miss and I went back to the clubhouse, we grabbed our bows. You can't be a Broken Bow and not have the irony of a death without one. Mine is a 50lb compound with my name etched across the top. It's easy to load, quick to fire, and it makes a statement.

Miss's bow *is* a statement. His long bow looks like something from a Robin Hood reenactment. The accuracy he has with it, though, is unparalleled. His road name is from the single miss he had in a competition against True. His shots are dead-on.

Removing it from the case he carries it in, he sets the waxed string, then tests the draw a few times.

"We'll take out the first two in style. They won't know what hit 'em." I motion to Cap and Raptor. "If you want to grab the other two, we'll let Soulless have some knife fun after we enter."

"And us?" Death questions, standing with Trigger.

"Easy. He's expecting me and you. We'll let him feel like he's getting what he asked for. There's an escape route that we sealed off a little while ago. If Trigger and Sinner come in through it, we'll have the advantage from behind. It's not a known thing, so I doubt King will expect it." Drawing in the dust on the truck hood, I show him where he'll come in, where he needs to go, and how they gain access. "King won't expect you to come with someone other than Curse, so with him in the hospital, we should have the advantage there. He'll expect us to be a man short."

Before taking the first shot, I ask if everyone's ready. With quick nods, Trigger and Sinner walk off, armed to the gills with guns and knives.

Checking on me, Miss walks over. "You good?"

"Yeah. I'm ready to rain down hell." Motherfucking King has been in control for far too long.

Smacking me on the back, he starts toward the edge of the building. Drawing back his bow, aiming at one of the agents, a slow whoosh sound is all that I hear as the bolt is released. Taking a look as he shoots, I see the agent he hit jerk slightly, but not fall to the ground immediately. He stares at the spot in his chest, then slowly collapses.

"That went right through," Cap says, thoroughly impressed as I'm nocking my own.

Aiming, releasing a deep breath, I let the wind carry the projectile to its intended target. Slamming into the back of the second agent, I watch him spin from the force. Mine packs a wallop even from this distance.

With the four other agents standing around and thoroughly confused as to the location of the hit, Raptor and Cap aim, taking out two each in quick succession.

"That was fun," Miss chuckles, full of mirth and excitement as he shoulders his bow and picks up his guns. "I'm in need of a celebratory round of head."

"You ain't gettin' that from any of us, fucker," Soulless tells him with a wide grin.

"I have a girl in mind, sick fuck. Though if you play with the rim right, I might let you do it twice."

"We ready to do this?" Smiling, I nod and laugh it off.

Soulless is taken aback by Miss, but I'm not. He'd take head from anyone if they did it right. Starting across the yard, I follow Miss as he calls out loudly, "Let's go fuck some shit up."

Chapter

Oubliette

We weren't the first here. That in itself excited King. As they sit upstairs causing a hubbub, I try to catch a glimpse of them.

"I'm glad you could join us, gentlemen," King greets loudly.

"We've waited a long time for you. You shouldn't keep your guests waiting, especially impatient ones," one man with a dark voice exclaims. I can't see him, but his tone speaks of his annoyance. I know the couch up there is set back pretty far, and I'm willing to bet he's reclined on one of them. I'm thankful. Thankful that the cages are devoid of other inhabitants. Thankful that we're down here alone to deal with the stress of being back here, and thankful that there's no other noises so we can hear their conversation.

"You were expected here an hour ago, King." The man's voice carries across the vacant space. Accented heavily, thicker on the consonants.

Working in the club, you get used to voices, accents, verbal cues and tones. This new voice is professional sounding. A true businessman. He's not kept waiting by *anyone*.

"Well, they are worth the wait. That, I promise you." King is smug. He's selling us to the highest bidder because he can. Grease a palm here, sell a body there. He's content to be dirty.

Prick.

Listening intently, I see them move to the edge of the railing and peering over. The men appear with King, along with one of his DEA flunkies. "They are a pretty pair. Biker trash you say? I wonder which *puta* will fetch the most?"

With a contemptuous glare, the other man expresses his deep hatred and disgust with us. Sneering, he turns his nose up. "*Piruja.*"

Whores.

Hookers.

Who the fuck do they think we are? We're not anyone's whores.

As a third approaches the railing, I'm taken aback by his good looks and relaxed attire, compared to his compatriots. Deciding that if we give them attitude, which will only fuel them on more, I do my best instead to concentrate on anything but them.

Staring down at my bloodstained hands, I'm still sickened by the sight. Feeling bile rise in my throat and an unceasing need to vomit up the death I've witnessed, I feel the room spin. I can't ignore the stain on the ground, though I wish I could, and the dark red that coats my hands is a constant reminder that Panna won't be there to joke with me when, or if, I return to the clubhouse.

I'm almost afraid to return to a place that's seen the death of someone so kind. I truly cared for Pandora. Reflecting on her in the best way, I think about how she cared for me when she didn't have to, and how she made me feel at home. She was the sweetest.

"Did you see your piece?" Jazzy asks me quietly, snapping me from my musings. Neither of us look to each other, we don't want to give them any indication we're interested in the glass that will save us.

"Yeah. You?"

"Totally. We'll be prepared if they think to step foot in here. I won't be someone's trash. I *won't* be made to sell my soul to save my body."

Eyeing that shard of glass, seeing it shimmer like a beacon, I memorize how far it is, how many steps until I get there, and how many times I'll have a chance to strike before they kill me. I'll gladly cut up my hands if it means we're not used as playthings to useless men.

Looking at Jazzy, she braids back her long, thick, jet-black hair and slings it over her shoulder, tying it with a hair elastic she had wrapped around her wrist. I'm kind of disappointed with myself for not having one too. I could desperately do with my long hair out of the way.

Venturing a look upstairs, I see the belligerent men toasting one another with glasses of wine and beer. They're so pleased with themselves.

Concentrating on each, memorizing their looks, I start with the loudest. The man that called us trash and whores. His dark hair, dark olive complexion, and tight dress shirt tells me he's someone that looks after himself. Though his bad hair is a hereditary issue that he can't avoid and control. He's compensating with a bad toupee. It's easy to see that with a stiff breeze it would be gone. He's probably South American. With that fancy, gaudy attire and the accent, maybe Columbian. He's someone who feels important. He feels powerful in this group. As powerful as you can be when you make people slaves to your whims.

The second, he's quiet. Reserved. Deadly. Even with the constant barbs from his buddy, he hasn't said another word beyond that first. His eyes are transfixed on us.

Gnawing at his lip, he contemplates how best to devour us. His hands grip the railing tightly as he imagines our bodies naked and in the throes of passion, or at the least, his hands wrapped around our necks as he murders us. I'll bet he gets off on it. He's deadly. *Him,* I'm afraid of. He won't slip up with us. He won't be like Nock.

He won't let my death bother him.

The third? To explain him by outfit, stature, and style, it feels wishy-washy. He's at least six feet tall, thick like a linebacker, a strong jaw, deep set dark eyes, and a look that tells of pain, contempt, heartlessness and maliciousness. Thing is, there's certain things about him that are...almost, but not quite recognizable. I can't place a finger on it, though. Staring down at us, eyeing us with lust and darkness, I feel sullied and uncomfortable.

"Do you know any of them up there?" I ask Jazzy.

Not venturing a gaze up, training her eyes to the concrete, she says, "You mean, other than the DEA that I know? No. The hulking black guy, and the crass Italian are not two I've seen before."

"I think he's South American."

"Same difference when you're an asshole."

True.

"Well, he gives me the heebie-jeebies." I flick a finger toward the Columbian. "He's too pompous to be scary. The other two, though, the one would use my veins as tooth floss, and the other would tattoo my dead stare on his chest to look at in the mirror each morning."

She leans forward, acting as if she's fucking with her shoe. "He is kinda familiar, though. Right? Or am I crazy?"

"I thought the same thing." Totally familiar. In a scary way, I'm fearful to find out the truth.

"Well, regardless, we have to find a way out of this. A way *not* to die."

"Agreed. Suggestions or thoughts on how we'll do that? King and his boyband members don't seem the kind that will trip up."

She grins in a wicked way, which tells me Jazzy has a dastardly evil plan. "Well, if it takes a bit of persuasion, we might have to...get close."

"Ugh."

"We are *piruja,* after all. We might as well use that to our advantage."

Great. Just what I wanted as a new memory in this building.

I hate this building. I wish to burn it to the fucking cement. I want dust on the wind kind of reminders and nothing further. No one should ever have to step foot in here again.

As we silently devise a plan, King tosses his glass toward the bedroom up there. The sound reverberates off the walls.

For some reason, King is pissed, yelling out, "Fuck! Why can't he just play the part he was trained for!"

King's tirade is loud. The only person I can think of that would piss anyone off that good is Lucius.

"Don't worry, *pendejo.* He's no match for us," the Columbian dude answers.

Cocky?

Misguided?

I doubt you're as dangerous as you put on. I think you're a man who works out in a gym, not one who's fighting on the streets for his life.

Lucius will wipe your ass with your toupee. You're done. I'm glad you'll stain this place.

The second man, man number two, is still sullen and silent. He looks down on us, but stays reserved and observant of the affair.

Man three. He's turned, walking down the stairs slowly and deliberately. It's a model perfected runway entrance if I'd ever seen one. Clicking his heavy boots on the stairs, his body arcs back and forth as he shifts. His hulking size covers the width of the space, railing to railing, in an imposing way.

Walking toward our containment, his face comes into view better. He's a good-looking man. Still dangerous and scary, but for an older guy, he's well-kempt. There are tattoos covering his arms, abstract and dark. From afar, it seemed that he was wearing a long shirt that covered to his wrists. Up close, as I sneak peeks, I see he's well-built and even scarier than I'd originally thought.

Not daring to raise our eyes his way, even as his feet come into view, Jazzy and I train our gazes on the shards that will save our lives, or end them if need be.

"I know who you are," he says, standing by the cage door, arms crossed and inspecting us.

We don't speak.

"Don't worry. Your secret is safe here, *coño*."

Wow. Calling me a cunt? This guy isn't gaining brownie points. Great. Now I'm having to use my very limited Mexican curse vocabulary.

Ignoring him further, I keep my mind on task. Shard. Life. Shard. Life. Anything else and I'm leaving Jazzy and I vulnerable. Too many have died because of me, so that won't fucking happen.

"You know he can't save you. It's not in his cards. It never was. He was too soft. Too *sweet*. I tried, though, you know?" Bending down, he leans on the cage's cross rails. "He would have been a god. Now he's less. Just another *puta madre* in my way." Reaching out to touch my hair, he strokes it between his fingers. I feel ill letting him put his hands on me. I still. I stay quiet.

"Fuck me!" King yells as he bounds down the stairs. Picking up an AK that was leaning on the railing, he checks the cartridge with a loud slam and click. "I guess I have to do everything myself. I can't leave torture and main to someone else because that fucker can't leave things alone," he mutters before crossing toward the security pad. King is furious.

"What's the issue, King?" The dark and deadly man asks as he stands back up.

King punches in a set of numbers. "It's nothing, really. It's that your sons have killed my guards outside and are walking toward the door with hand grenades and C-4."

King gives us a seedy glare. "Don't worry, ladies." Hearing the door to our cage unlock, King snaps, "We're bringing you to where it's safe."

Shard.

Life.

Shard.

Death.

No matter what he says, I don't feel safe in his company. King with a large gun removes my ability to feel safe. Knowing that he's about to walk in, gun in hand, I act as if I'm scrambling away from the door, away from him, but I'm really shifting over to my glass. Jazzy does the same.

"Mind helping out?" he asks the other man.

Leaning on the cage, right by my glass, I don't dare look up. I don't want him to know what I'm doing, that I'm looking for my lifeline.

"Not my issue, *cabrón*."

"That's fine, *Jefe*." Grabbing the door to our room, he slides in, tough and tumble. "I'll have my boys help then. This'll cost you, though."

"*Nothing* costs me. It costs you, *diablo*."

Halting, King stills for a moment before advancing on me. "Time to go, Oubliette. Your man is on the way. I'd hate to see you hurt because of him blowing a hole in the wall where you are." Reaching to grab my shoulder, King presses his fingers deep in my skin.

Without choice, I rise. I rise with the shard in my hand. Moving as he asks, doing what he instructs, the gun of his causes me pause. He could turn it on Jazzy if I attack him with my glass.

I wait.

"Henerd!" he yells up the stairs. "Get your ass down here and grab the other bitch."

Standing tall, stiff fingers in my shoulder, I slip the glass into my pocket.

"Move," King snaps at me. "We're relocating you for your safety. I really wish you'd understand I'm the good guy, Oubliette." Stepping to the door of the cage, involuntarily, I look the dark and dangerous man in the eye. Piercing, his gaze is trained on King. With a look like that, I'd hate to be on the receiving end.

"Don't turn your back on that one, King. She has your death planned out." With a slow blink, he drags his eyes toward the pocket where I'm housing my weapon. A smile creeps across his face before he turns his eyes my way and winks.

"I have the gun. I think I have the upper hand, *Jefe*."

Walking off toward the upper deck, taking the steps heavily, he leaves me to King's control.

"I don't think that gun will save you from her, King. Keep wary," he states with a sinister smile, looking again at my pocket.

My heart races, my body vibrates with the fear of being outed, and I do everything I can to still my features. Don't give it away. Don't show fear. Don't give away that you're dying inside with the thought of hurting another *again*. Don't break down.

As the agent bypasses us on the stairs, presumably to grab Jazzy, I walk where King directs. Edging me up, he pushes me forward quickly. Touching the first, then the next, his gun is close enough that I feel it resting on my back. His fingers are so tight in my shoulder, I know there'll be immediate bruising.

"Fucking move, woman!" he yells. As we move to the top stair, an explosion rocks the building.

Chapter

Oubliette

Running up the rest of the way, King pushes me forward ahead of him in a rush. "Jesus fucking Christ!" Hitting the top stair, he roughly guides me to the couch I'd once occupied.

That was before.

That was when I hated Lucius.

That was before I learned he was—is, fantastic.

"Take a fucking seat and do me a favor—don't move."

As shots ring out, with his gun trained on the men below, I hide on the far side of the leather. King spins on his heels, concentrating on the intruders.

Glancing around the couch, I watch with shock as the professional asshole in the million-dollar suit takes a hit to the head. His body spins and falls fast, the meticulous outfit twisted from the force.

With his eyes turned my way, the vacant look reminds me of Nock.

What did I do in a past life to deserve this? This consistency of death? Maybe I should embrace it and let it swallow me whole.

I could take it and let it fuel me toward my escape.

But could I?

Knowing that running now constitutes a bullet like the million-dollar guy, what choice do I have but to stay low?

Feeling a pinch in my side, I'm reminded that the shard is in my pocket. I contemplate attacking King while his back is turned, but that again requires me to leave the protection of the couch. Taking in the whole room, seeing one of the DEA agents take a hard hit to the chest, he harrumphs and falls to the floor. That leaves King, the not so fancy guy, and one more agent. Not-so-fancy is leaning on the far wall at the entrance to the bedroom with a beer in hand, more interested in something on his phone than the gunfire. He's very calm in this situation. Aloof and uninterested in the destruction.

With the agent pinned down on the right by another shooter, one I can't see, the shots are consistent and deadly. As one squarely nails the agent in the head, I wince as the splatter coats the room surrounding him. He had no chance. Yeah, King has the *law* on his side, but the law doesn't give you an invisible shield to protect you from those with better aim.

Settling behind the couch, attempting to decrease my target, I hope for safety. That's when I think about Jazzy. Where is she? Is she safe? Is she caught in the crossfire? Shifting slightly, hoping to see down below, dark scuffed boots halt my advance, blocking my view. Standing where he is, the not-so-fancy guy is relatively clean—no marks and no bloodstains. He hasn't sustained damage. Yet.

"Going somewhere?"

I don't feel it requires a reply, so I keep my mouth shut.

"Don't move," he says coolly, sipping again once more on that sweat drenched bottle.

"Don't tell me what to do," I say. My voice is strong, and the comment sterner than I'd thought to reply. Knowing that the man before me is the scariest of them all, I wonder when I grew balls the size of watermelons.

"Fine. Stand up if you're so tough," he chides.

Steeling my spine, hoping that my body doesn't shake with fear and give away my inherent unease of him, I spit out, "I'm not tough. I'm only looking for my friend."

Guzzling back more beer, he sets the empty bottle on the table. With a wipe to his mouth with the back of his hand, he shrugs. "The gunfire is pretty much done, *Princesa*. Come out." Holding out a hand, his menacing form looms above me. "I won't hurt you. It wouldn't do me any good." That's when a shot hits his leg. I see the bullet pierce his pants, and the blood slowly starts to stain the material. It doesn't seem to faze him. With his hand still out, waiting on me, I consider my options. Not great I'm afraid. Gritting my teeth, I rise.

With the assistance of the menacing man, standing to my full height, my tiny size compared to his hulking form, it brings me only to his chest. Laying a finger under my chin, raising my face to meet his, he smiles. It's not creepy like Nock, but not really welcoming either. I stay silent as he peruses my face and mutters, "*Guera.*"

Reaching his other hand out, fiddling with my blonde hair that loosely rests across my forehead, I still like a deer in headlights. Not-so-fancy guy up close is a scary. His body is strong, his face is youthful, even as his jet-black hair is peppered with gray. His bright eyes tell me he sees everything. With a stiff grin, his lip turns up as he blows out a haughty laugh. "You're tough, aren't you? Just a little scorpion waiting to strike." Laying a hand on my pocket, he slowly pulls out the shard of glass. "You won't need this." Lifting it free and with ease, he's taken my only protection.

Feeling uncomfortable with the exchange, knowing he has what could kill me, I take a step back. His smile doesn't decrease with the motion. On the contrary, it ramps up. He enjoys my defiance.

Noticing the silence, that the gunfire has ceased, I look to King. His body armor is covered in stains, a hole in his arm is leaking, blood is smeared across his forehead, and there's a worn, weary look in his eyes.

"*Jefe*, I see you're still standing." Looking at his partners splayed out on the floor, I track as his eyes pause on one in particular. "I see Jorge and my men didn't fare so well."

"They didn't know how to duck." Crossing his arms, thickening out his form, scary guy hides the shard. His whole character makes his comment contemptuous. King may think he's running something here, but this man *is* the power.

"Do you think it's time we got on with the introductions? After all, we've built up the surprise for so long." King grins with a sense of control. He thinks he still holds the ace. Even as he's now outnumbered by bad guys, King has a false sense of security. Honestly, I'm rooting for the bad guys.

Not rising to the poke, not bothered by King's obvious attempt to control the situation, he shrugs and offers a look of simple boredom. "By all means. I'm sure they're dying to find out what the fuck you're up to, *cabrón*."

"Let's start, *Hector*." King holsters his gun and yells throughout the space, "Come on up! We have something to discuss." He smirks. "You might as well bring everyone with you, Lucius. At least they can have a beer and patch up."

Pointing to the blood pouring out of King's shoulder, Hector walks to the fridge. "Might want to take your own advice, Magnus." Pulling free a beer, he uncaps it and guzzles a monster mouthful.

"Yeah, suppose I should." Grabbing a bottle of tequila off the counter, King pops the top and pours it across his arm. He winces slightly, but shakes it off and swigs directly from the bottle.

Hearing the heavy footfalls on the stairs, I nervously watch for the owners of the noise. I'm watching for Jasmine and Bennett, sure, but more than that, I'm afraid of *not* seeing them.

As each come into view, I smile, knowing that even though Death took damage, he's alive and well. Jazzy is helping him as he limps through a bullet to the leg. Cresting the stairs, helping her brother toward the couch, I run over to assist.

Helping them the last of the way, "I'm so glad you're okay."

Eyeing the not-so-fancy guy and King, Bennett's scowl deepens. "You good?" he asks.

"Yeah, I'm good." Shaking my head a little too vigorously, I smile the fakest smile I can muster.

As he flops down heavily on the leather, Jazzy asks, "Is there a kit here?"

"Yeah. Hang on, let me look," I say, starting off to look in the kitchen.

"It's in the cabinet under the sink, Obi."

Breathing a sigh of relief, I don't dare turn and look at Lucius. If I do that, I know that I'll never get to Bennett. If I see damage on him, or see that smile of his looking my way, I'll break down and run into his arms.

Pulling the plastic box out from under the sink, I turn toward the couch. Still not looking at Lucius, I cross the space while clicking open the first-aid kit. "Here," I say, pulling out gauze and alcohol.

Bennett winces when his punctured leg rests on the cushions, and as Jazzy takes the offered aids, she smiles, giving me a wicked wink. "Go check on him."

Filling my lungs with air, I turn and blow it out. Glad to see him alive and well, I smile with relief. As tears of joy threaten my eyes, I take in the sight of Lucius. His face is stern, his jaw rigid, and I'd bet money he's grinding his poor teeth together. His eyes are focused, trained on the man that King called Hector, and there's blood trickling down the arm that holds his gun. As I open my mouth to say something, he grins, telling me with his eyes to ignore it.

Moving around the couch, walking toward him, Lucius holds out that arm—yet his eyes don't leave the not-so-fancy guy. As I tuck into his chest and his arm comes around to hug me tight, I feel him breathe into my hair and whisper low, "I'd like you to go sit by Death and Jazzy. If I tell you to run, don't hesitate, Obi."

Nodding into his chest, his lips leave me and I move out of his embrace.

Sitting down on the couch, I look around at our inhabitants. Sucking down on a beer, leaning on the damaged railing, Hector's gaze is trained on Lucius. With awe and spite, they both take in the other. They're not only dangerous and ominous looking, but in a way, relieved.

"What the fuck! Tell me what the fuck's goin' on. Right now!" Joining our cadre, another man shouts as he rises up the stairs.

"Cap," Lucius calls out with a level voice.

"Don't fucking Cap me, Lucius. What the fuck is *he* doing here?"

Storming across the space, he gets right in Hector's face. Cap, Lucius, and Hector resemble each other so much.

"Son," Hector calmly greets, squaring off against him.

Raising a gun, pointing it at his temple, Cap scowls. "I could pull this trigger and not be upset at all."

"I would expect nothing less." Pushing his head into the muzzle, he makes it rest even tighter against his skin. "You've grown up, Codero."

His voice is menacing. "*That* happens when you're thrown in foster. *That* happens when your family tosses you away. *That* happens when you grow up on the streets without a father or family to guide you."

Opening his mouth to yell further, Lucius interrupts him with a growl. "Cap. Stand down, man."

"Fuck off, *brother.* He deserves this and more." Cap is livid. "I could click this and bathe myself in your blood, and I wouldn't lose a moment's sleep."

"Don't hesitate on my account," Hector taunts him. He doesn't think that his son has the balls to do it. If he's anything like Lucius, he's thought wrong. They're more than ready to kill.

As I watch the interaction, waiting on someone to crack, I anticipate that either someone will wrestle the gun away, or assist, and click the trigger. But it doesn't come.

"Cap." As another steps up the stairs, I'm blown away at his beauty. He looks more like a rap god than a biker. With his side shaved head, afro tied tight in a thick braid, bright caramel eyes and a teardrop tattoo under his right eye, he's scary in a gorgeous way.

"He deserves this and more, Troy." Man, I'm getting so confused by the players in this game. Multiple names depending on who's talking. I need a playbook.

The Troy guy pipes up, "It's not about right or wrong. Grim did what he had to. Ask your brother. It's all *that* fucker's fault," he growls as he points to King.

Raising the bottle of tequila, the wound in his arm continuously leaks. King is smiling through the whole altercation, feeling in charge and without remorse for this end.

Eyeing the roomful of testosterone, I know it won't take long for this to come to blows once more. Lucius hasn't pulled his sights from King. Cap holds the gun to Hector, his friend that's just entered still holds a large gauge gun, and as Miss walks up behind him with a bow strung across his back, in his hand is a menacing looking weapon too.

Nothing about this is going to go well for someone.

Stepping across the space, ignoring the interactions, Miss appears beside me. "Doin' good, little lady?"

I shrug. "I need a drink."

Smiling, he unhooks his bow from his shoulder and sets it at our feet, then hands Bennett a gun from his waistband. "No new holes?"

"I'm good, Miss. Thanks," Bennett tells him. The tension-filled air makes my skin itch, but I stay alert. Lucius is on edge, and the last thing he needs to worry about is me.

"If shit goes down, don't worry." Miss grins, tapping his bow. "I got ya, Oubliette."

If?

No.

When shit goes down.

Looking back at the players, Cap and Hector are in a stalemate. "You're gonna take that gun from my temple, kid." Hector chides.

"Tell me why I should, *Dad.*"

"Because I hold your freedom," King states, deadpan.

"Bullshit. We kill you, then we can go right on going with the way life was. No King, no problem," Lucius states, cool as a cucumber.

Turning his head slightly, Hector levels a look at Lucius. "It's not as simple as that, kid."

"Bullshit. You're just saving your ass," Troy snaps.

While shock courses the faces of the brothers and the friend, the rest of us are at a loss. We don't know the whole story.

Resting his hand on the gun, Hector takes the pistol from Cap.

The room stills as the air is sucked out.

"I'm lost," Jazzy says quietly. Damn right we are.

Glimpsing out of the corner of my eye that Lucius has pulled out his gun, Miss picks up his bow quickly. With cool regard, he orders, "Obi. Duck, please."

B usta
Vibrating.

Seething with unfettered anger.

A need to destroy.

I eye King. He's too smug.

He's known all along. I see it. He's *known* all along how this was going to end, where we'd lose. He holds our fates in his hands and our clubs have been the tools.

Yeah. I knew where Cody was and I'd left him to grow on his own, even as his club and mine started to cross paths. I'd had no interaction with them, so it was easy to avoid that altercation.

When we were kids, I'd done everything I could to keep him from this bullshit. Even me taking that plea deal and becoming King's flunky, I'd done it all to keep Cody from King's manipulations. I figured that he was better off with street gangs and juvie than with me in his world. I was dragged into this shit and I didn't want him growing up with that.

Every time I think of all that King's taken from me—from us, my blood boils.

I know the truth. I know Cap and his club has been dirty, and that there's been some issues with the local clubs and these 'upstart' punk riders, but I thought he was out of King's grasp and not in his sights. It appears I was wrong.

"You've lied before, King. What makes it that we should believe your lies now?" Cap asks.

Raising my gun, I point it at King, watching for Cap's reaction.

"I have cells already picked out for all of you at a maximum security facility that would make Guantanamo seem like Club Med. That's right, isn't it, Hector?"

I look for the truth of it in his eyes. His stance tells me that King is telling the truth.

Not thinking if it's the right or wrong thing to do, I take a shot, hitting King in the other shoulder.

"Jesus Christ!" King curses.

"Be glad I aimed for your shoulder." Holstering my gun, I feel a sense of relief for causing him damage personally. If I could, I'd shoot him a hundred times for every time he caused me pain. For every time he destroyed a piece of my life. When he turned me into his weapon, when he thought it was his right as a *man of the law*.

"Nice shot," Rap chuckles, raising his gun. Popping off a shot, he too leaves a bullet in King.

Hitting his right leg, he falls to his knees, breathing heavily through the pain. "I left files with the appropriate authorities. My bosses know what's been going on with these clubs. Without my help, none of you will survive. One press of a button and you're all gone. Every fucking last one of you." Raising himself back up, the smug look has been replaced with one of fear. Fear that his ruse has ended and he has no leverage.

Sneering and leveling a look of disdain, Hector answers King. "Their families are better out of your grasp, *puta*. If you die, no leverage."

He's right.

"So why come to California then, Hector? You knew I was planning an ambush. You knew I was looking to leverage all the clubs further and it was for your gain! Help me. Help me to keep you in your position, *Jefe*."

King's power is failing. He knows he's outgunned, outmanned and outmaneuvered. The clubs have taken back the power. That's why he didn't want us going legit. That's why he put pressure on True and the other club members, he wanted to leverage us into his debt for years to come. A war would do that. A war makes him money.

Looking to Miss, I give him a wink. I wish I'd brought my bow up with me, but this will be poetic.

Raising it, knocked fast and released, the bolt zips through King's shoulder. Lodging in the wood of the bar behind him, pinning King in place, his smug, powerful attitude is replaced with one of fear.

"You have a right to be fearful, Magnus," our father states with a smugness of his own. "I *know* what you were planning." Stepping closer, he approaches King. "I've known all along. But my sons, you had them hidden quite well. Until two years ago, I had no idea how to connect with them." Looking over his shoulder at us, Cap and I, Hector continues. "You thought that deporting me to Mexico was the best thing for *you*. Having me in a place of power in the cartel would be an asset to *you*. That me running the *Alta Noche* would be in the DEAs favor. So, for that I have to thank you, Magnus. It gave me a chance to see how they'd grown, how powerful they'd become. To see that without me, they became the strong men I expected they would be."

"You're a part of Alta Noche?" Cap questions.

"I'm not a *part* of Alta, I *am* Alta Noche. I am the *Jefe*, the king, I am the power. Nothing happens in SoCal and North Mexico without my knowledge." He turns to me. "I know everything, Busta."

Well fuck.

Leader of the flesh trade in New York becomes the cartel boss of the flesh trade in Mexico because of DEA intervention. That would be a bestselling story if I'd ever heard one.

Hector steps closer to King with a look of satisfaction. "Magnus, any last requests?"

Wincing through the pain, King tries to pull the fletched arrow. "I should've listened to Hart. He thought I'd picked the wrong club to pull apart."

"Yes, you should've listened." Placing his hand on King's chin, he raises his face up to meet his. Pulling free something from his pocket, Hector swipes it across King's neck, quickly, before thrusting it in his chest.

Stepping back as King gurgles, Hector walks directly to the fridge. Looking over his shoulder as if nothing is amiss, he raises a beer to me. "Want one?"

Peering at King, I see him gasping for air, trying to cover the wound in his neck. Even as the long shard of glass is lodged in his chest, I'm stunned into silence as I watch the instrument of my twisted life dies before my eyes. It's poetic justice that Grim has reaped from the man that sowed his own demise.

As the light leaves King's eyes, and his last breath rattles out, my father places a beer in my view. "Here."

Holding it up, I grasp the neck and swill it back in refreshing gulps. The cool liquid drains the fire in my soul. The shroud of every dirty deed, every step that King orchestrated, it all falls away.

"So..." Pausing for dramatics, Cap chirps, "What do we do now, *dear ol' Dad?*" Hearing the distinct sound of a gun slipping into a holster, I turn and smile that Cap has picked up the bottle of tequila that King had been slugging back. Pouring a glassful, he takes a seat over the arm of the vacant couch beside the one Death currently occupies.

Now that the dust has settled and there's no exchange of gunfire, a strange calm comes over us as a group. Holding the beer that my father offered, I feel a sense of relief.

That is, until he talks.

"We need to find middle ground between Alta Noche and the clubs. My business is your business, *boys.*" He states it as if it's fact. Law. If Hector thinks we're all just going to fall in-line with him now that King isn't twisting us up, he has another thing coming.

Cap pops his lips. "Not to be disrespectful, but I'm going to be. You're an asshole if you think that I'll do that, or that my club wants anything to do with Alta. You haven't been a father, and you sure as shit aren't my god damn leader, *Jefe.*"

I agree with my brother. "Gotta side with Cap. Not happenin.'"

"Yeah, not us either," Bennett states as he rises up on his elbows before standing up weakly. Jazzy moves to help right him, but he shrugs off her assistance.

Surrounded by enemies, leaning on the bar, right by King's dead form, the leader of the Alta Noche, our father, looks the part of an all-powerful cartel boss, dead body and all. "You know, I'd hoped this would be easy, that we'd find middle ground. It seems I was wrong, *pobericto*."

Laughing, not in a funny way, but in a sinister 'I'll cut your heart out' kind of way, Cap rises from the couch quickly. "Yeah, we haven't been your *poor little sons* for years."

Taking my eyes from Hector and looking to my brother, I see that he's on the cusp of killing. He looks as I feel. I don't really know everything he's been through, so being called *son* by a man that abandoned and deserted him in juvie to deal with whatever he came across in the past ten years, it could be a trigger.

I'm not the only one who sees the change in Cap. As his face reddens, his stance tightens and his hand grips the glass to the breaking point. He's holding his murderous tendency by a thin thread. One small move and he'll easily kill our father. The king of hell will find out how wrong his intentions are.

Walking over, tapping Cody on the shoulder, Raptor tries to gain his attention. "Code, not the time to worry about it, man."

With a blink, like flicking a switch, Cap becomes his freewheeling guy once more. Shrugging off the touch, cracking a wide smile—a devious one—Cap snaps out of his darkness. "Not to burst your bubble, but we won't comic book team up with Alta Noche, *Jefe*."

Looking to me, knowing he's lost with Cap, my father is expecting a better answer. I state it straight. "You already have our answer. I'm not changing."

He won't rule us.

Pushing off the bar, he sets his bottle on the counter. "Well, it seems the sons feel they're above my control, that I can't pressure you into anything. You sure about that?"

Why am I suddenly at a point that I feel we're still missing a piece of this puzzle?

With a serious tone, a dark look and a tight jaw, he growls, "You will do as I need. I have more connections than you can imagine. More hands in more pies. More politicians that don't want their mysterious business trips halted, that don't want their fat cat pockets to run dry. That without my cartel, they wouldn't have money to fuel their drug wars, gun wars, and money to assist with the homeless situation. Oh, you're all so naive if you feel I didn't orchestrate it all."

Coming to terms with his ideals, wondering if he really would have us under his thumb for good, I decide quickly what I need to do to fix it.

I never thought this would happen. But it has. Here I am, using what tools I have in my arsenal to fight a war I don't wish to be a part of. The last piece I ever thought I'd use.

Reaching in my wallet, pulling it out, I flash it at my father. "Hector Alonzo Guierra, as a sworn officer of the DEA, I'm placing you under arrest for the murder of DEA agent Magnus King, for the trafficking of drugs, human trafficking, and the charge of gun running across state and federal lines." I know he won't go for it, nor will he take it standing by idly.

Gunfire is inevitable.

Knowing Grim, knowing he can kill with pretty much any object, I pull out my gun. "I won't read you your rights, as I doubt you'll make it that far."

No reply.

No answer.

I feel the tension in the room shift another degree. Out of the corner of my eye, I watch Oubliette. Sitting by Jazzy, the two of them move toward the bedroom for protection. She's slowly taking her time, not wanting to be seen as a moving target. Taking her friend with her, I see Bennett readying his gun. Knowing this will not be easy, I look at the ammo surrounding our father. A bottle, a plastic cup, a gun—which is out of character for him. King is still being held up by the arrow that Miss lodged in his shoulder, so that weapon is available too.

"I won't make it easy," Hector finally says.

"Yeah. Didn't think you would."

As he moves, we're all on guard, preparing for the attack. I see the door to the room close, placing the girls out of sight, and Bennett steps up beside me. Miss is to the left, a bolt at the ready, while Raptor pulls free a few knives from his pockets.

It still won't be enough. Not if we don't strike first.

I look down at one of the dead DEA agents sprawled out in front of me. Bending low, grasping the cuffs looped at his backside, I pull them free.

"Last chance," I say, flicking the cuffs.

Crossing his arms and facing off with the men surrounding him, Grim grins and waves us on. "I'm ready to dance."

O**ubliette**
 "What the hell am I missing in this picture?" Jazzy angrily whispers as we shut and lock the door.

"Which part?" I'm sure it's the whole thing, because in all honesty, I need a playbook too.

Moving to the unmade bed, screwing up her face in disgust, she tosses the blanket across. Hopping up, sitting cross-legged and as far from the door as we possibly can, I think about it all.

She cracks her neck. "Just give me whatch got. I'll see if I can fill in the blank spots."

Fine. Taking a seat beside her, I try out the CliffsNotes version. "Lucius and Cody are brothers. Grim or Hector is their dad, and he seems to be the leader of a cartel from Mexico. Got me so far?"

"Yep, I had that, but who's the other guy? Rap?"

"I'm at a loss too. I have the feeling he's known them since they were kids, though."

"And that Cody. I'd rate him on the same level as Trigger, but without the angst."

"Who are you rating against that Trigger guy?" A dark voice rings out.

"Trigger?" Looking around the space, I don't see him. "Where the hell are you?"

"Over here," he groans. Lifting a metal grate on the floor, his head is visible as he pokes it through. Running over to help, Jazzy and I hold the heavy lid as high as we can so that he and another guy can rise through it.

Why didn't I see it last time? Shit. If I'd known it was here, would I have had enough strength to hold it open? Probably not.

"What's goin' on, girls?" Trigger asks as he hops through, finally standing upright. Continuing to hold the lid, we watch as the second man passes through.

Jazzy quips sarcastically, "Oh, you know. Guns, bows drawn, knives, family squabble and dead DEA. Just a lovely day in paradise."

"Well, bows I get, guns—sure, and a family squabble is always expected. But who's having fun with knives without me?" With a monster smile, the newcomer seems giddy to get in on the action. "Pop the door. Let me go have some fun."

"Who's this guy again?" Jazzy asks Trigger.

"Jasmine, Sinner. Sinner, Oubliette. Sinner's with Heartless, recently appointed to the position of president."

"Recently?" I ask.

"Soulless is downstairs. Two to the chest." His voice is devoid of emotion, but you can't miss that he's trying to act tough. I can see that he's upset. He's sad. With a throat clearing sound, he palms a blade. "So, who's going to open the door for me? I'm not staying in here like a bitch."

"I will," I tell him. I haven't heard gunshot or scuffling sounds, but it's not like they're having a tea party, which means the danger is still out there.

I move to the door. "You comin'?" he asks Trigger.

"Fuck yeah. Like you can do this alone, pussy."

Well that's a first. Not only because Trigger is talking, more than one or two words, but the last man I heard call him a pussy had a week in traction for their troubles.

"Lead on," Sinner says, laughing.

I can't believe they both willingly want to go out there. But if they want it, who am I to stop them. Opening the door, I peer out. Flanking each other, Lucius, Cody, Bennett, and Miss each have a weapon drawn. As the two men join the others, I look at Lucius's father. He's calm. His whole demeanor shows that he believes he has the upper hand against well-armed men.

Closing the door quick, I lock it once more. "How's it going out there?" Jaz asks.

"Hard to say. They have the upper hand."

"How is it hard to say if they have the upper hand?"

"Something tells me that man has a trick or two up his sleeve. If not, do you think Bennett and Lucius would still be standing there staring at him?"

"Shit."

Laughing, I pat the edge of the bed as I take a seat. "Come on. I have the feeling we'll be here a while."

Chapter

B<u>usta</u>

If wishes were Harleys, I'd need a garage full to fulfill what I need out of life. To fix the wrongs against us and to make things right.

As the side door opened, I was ready to tell Obi to shut the fucking thing and hide as far away as she could. Seeing Trigger and Sinner walk out, though, with guns and knives at the ready, I think it finally put everything into perspective with my father.

"There's no good way out of this."

He's outnumbered.

Swinging the cuffs, twirling them on my finger, I watch as Hector sees that the odds are no longer in his favor.

Pushing off the bar, taking a walk to the railing, he looks over. "You know, this building was state-of-the-art. The *puta* and *guera* that came through here were of the finest quality. I never worried if what you sent me would perform or sell well." He turns back to face me. "So now you want me to give in? You think I'll turn myself over to you?"

He pauses.

Staring me in the eye, then looking to Cody and Rap, he says, "What if I offer you more profit? What if I gave you more control? Would that entice you to keep up our arrangements?"

"I think I speak for all of us—no." Stepping toward him, I know that my brother and these men have my back, but I still don't trust Hector.

"Fine. Lucius, you've done me proud, niño. You're more than I imagined you could be. I'll relent." With me close enough to clip the first bracelet on, I slap it to his outstretched wrist. As I move to link the second, with a move faster than I anticipated, he slips under my arm and holds his clipped arm to my neck. What a stupid fucking move.

He speaks low and close. "I never wanted this, remember that. I always loved you."

176

"Funny way to show it," I state through a strained and exposed throat. With gritted teeth, Hector turns me to face those that stand against him.

Switching tactics, looking for them to switch sides, Hector makes a try for my brother. "Cap, Raptor, I'll give you control over San Bern if you let me go." Bold move. Cap and I haven't been close, so it's a smart approach.

Raising his eyes to meet mine, Cody almost looks like he'll give in. "Nah, I'm good. We have enough with the legal shit. We don't need someone else's problems."

"I can make you fucking rich! No more dime-store operations. You'd be a fucking king." Hector is grasping at straws as he turns to Sinner.

He twirls a butterfly knife back and forth. "I'm good. Thanks, but fuck you."

Hector's running out of options. He may have me in a precarious position with the cuff pressed against my throat, but I'm not afraid. He's learning that loyalty is the currency—not fear with excessive stacks of bullshit.

Knowing he's losing, knowing that his chance at keeping the clubs in his pocket is waning, my father digs the cuff end in deeper. The edge isn't sharp, but he's pushing it deep enough to cause pain. I don't mind, though, as I know I still have the advantage.

Miss.

His bow is drawn, and all it would take is a quick nod from me for him to let loose.

But I don't want that. At least, not yet. I want Hector desperate.

"How long had you known?" I ask.

"Known?" He pushes the link harder, making it difficult to swallow. "I'd known that King had you hidden and out of my grasp for years. But I knew that the taste for club life would be too hard for you both to pass up. You'd turn up sooner or later."

Stepping forward, gun drawn with a deadliness in his expression, Cody is beyond pissed off. "Why did it matter where we were if you weren't even in the country? You were leading the Mexican underground. You had no use for us. We weren't important. Otherwise, you'd have contacted us earlier. Don't lie, it's not a good look on you." Lowering his gun, Cody fires. Shooting the ground by our father's feet, he smiles. "Shit, I missed. I need to work on my aim it seems."

I can't see his face, but Hector stiffens. He didn't expect that.

"You won't have a second chance, child. Don't fuck up next time or someone could get hurt." With a swift move, Hector draws the gun from my side. Firing, he shoots Raptor between the eyes.

Without a second thought, Miss let's his arrow fly. I feel the breeze of it as the flight nicks my cheek. The strength behind the shot is so forceful that Hector's body flies back, taking me with him in the process. The cuff catches in my neck, sticking in as I fall backward onto Hector's now slumped and lifeless body.

I can't move. The weight of his arm and the cuff in the position it is. If I shift, I have the ability to cause myself more damage.

"Shit!" I hear Miss yell as he runs over. "Fuck, man, I didn't think that was gonna happen." Inspecting my neck, turning his head slightly to peer around the edge of the cuff and where it's stuck, he says, "Dude, I need the key to uncuff his ass first. Someone root through that dead ass and find the key."

I open my mouth to speak, but the way the cuff sits it's pressing on my Adam's apple too tightly.

"Shut up, dumbass. Let us get the cuffs off before you try to speak," Cody snaps, bending down beside me. Looking above me, he fixes his eyes on our sperm donor. "Fuckin' wicked shot. Damn near perfect," he states loudly, knowing that Miss will hear him.

Miss returns with the key. "It *was* perfect," he states. Reaching around my head, grabbing the dead hand, he releases it from the cuff. "Let's not take it out yet. Stand up first so we can see the damage."

Blinking to show I agree, Cody helps me rise. As Miss holds the cuff in place, Cody pulls out a chair, close enough that I can sit.

"Okay, man, let's look at this."

Calming my breathing, staying as still as I can, the cold steel shifts as Miss tries to find the best way to remove it. "Can someone grab that gauze?" Turning his head this way and that, I wish it didn't hurt to speak or I'd joke that his ass isn't my type. He's fuckin' close enough to kiss that his breath is moving my beard.

When he's finally satisfied with how to take it out, he breathes, "Okay. Busta, I need to pull it back in one move. Take a deep breath then swallow. I'll take it out as you swallow."

With a blink, I respond that I got it.

"One, two...three."

Feeling the hard metal as it pulls back, the final suck noise as it pops free is the last thing I feel before he places the gauze against the wound.

"Well, that went easier than I thought," Miss states as he holds it tight to the wound. With it packed tight, wrapping it around my throat and tucking in the end, he steps back to inspect his handiwork. "That was a perfect shot."

I try my voice. "Yep." It hurts a bit, but it's tolerable. Looking behind me at the deadened eyes of my father and King, I find it freeing. It means the end of an era for us. We're released from their rule. The Alta Noche. The DEA. The power they held over us. We can start the way we want without their intervention.

As I sit there, contemplating the future, the door to the bedroom opens.

"Lucius!" Obi screams, running across the space. Tucking her under my arm, it feels perfect. Nothing is wrong in this moment, everything is right.

When her friend Jazzy shifts to help Death, giving him an arm to lean on and bringing him back to the couch, her eyes go to the dead body. Raptor, who has been my brother's best friend for as long as I can remember, is the one man I didn't think we'd lose today.

"Code?" I call out.

Clearing his throat, swallowing back the tears that threaten to take control, Cody works to contain his distress. "Yeah. What do ya need, Lu?"

"We'll help take care of him. He deserves it and more." I may not have seen Raptor or Cap in years, but Rap was as close to me as a brother could be when we were young.

Crossing his friend's arms and rising off the floor, Cap pulls in his emotions. "How do you figure we play this out?"

"I have an idea on that," Miss says with a grin. "But I think we need more booze for this."

When Miss has an idea, I know it's a good one.

"Run it down," I say before we all quiet and listen to his plan.

B <u>usta</u>

"So, you're telling me that this—" he huffs, swinging his arms wide, "is because of a Homeland Security agent on the take, a dirty DEA team, and the Alta Noche cartel? And that you, the law-abiding *outlaw* biker clubs, cleaned up the city of L.A. for us? Out of the goodness of your civic duty to the law? Does that about sum it up?"

"Pretty much," I tell him.

Deputy Director of the FBI in the Los Angeles District, John Curry, sits outside the warehouse in a makeshift command post, going over the details of the fight, the deaths, and the moments that led to this. My voice is still hoarse, but giving my details—right down to the part where I've been an agent for years—under deep cover, I gave up everything I had on Johnathan Hart, Magnus King, and my father, Hector Alonso Guierra. I explained the location of my intel that is stored on databases, the details of the various logs regarding the flesh trade, contacts, and any other pertinent information that can help keep us out of the line of fire.

After we'd devised the plan and set out about enacting it, Sinner and Miss left with the body of Raptor and Soulless, as they didn't need to be a part of this. Trigger and Cap stuck around with me, and the girls took Death to their repairman to fix up his leg. The less here to question, the less to fuck up the story. And with Trigger's track record, and Cap's credentials—which I quickly found out—we had verified accounts from real life, all-American heroes. It was airtight, substantiated information on the biggest cartel boss and who he was in league with.

"Well, we'll have to verify it all. We'll need to give agent King and his deceased team the benefit of the doubt until I can further confirm it all." Sipping at his fifth coffee since sitting with us, agent Curry processes it all. "I don't have anything to charge you with directly—yet.

But I'm sure there's something we'll find in the future." Standing up, pacing the space that the four of us and a few of his agents occupy, you'd swear that he's hoping to find a reason to arrest us all. We are a motley bunch after all.

I didn't know the extent of Trigger and Cap's military involvement before, but now I have a newfound appreciation for their skills and years of service. They look the true part of regimented soldiers, while the FBI in their pristine dress shirts and vests seem more like pencil pushers than Federal police.

Trigger, I've found out, was Special Forces, and Cap was black ops—that's all he'll say.

It's enough for me to know both are men you don't mess with. Even as young as they are, the two of them command attention from the agents in our midst and their answers gather weight with the Special Agent Curry.

Receiving a call, Agent Curry answers. "Yeah...Of course, sir...No...No, I don't believe there's an immediate threat...Yes, I think it can be contained...Of course...Yes, but—" He pauses as he listens to the person on the other end, staring at me. "Yes, sir. Thank you." With that, the other person hangs up. Pocketing his phone, he says to me, "Don't go far." Curry sets his newly emptied cup on the table and starts for the door of the tent. "We'll be in touch—Agent Guierra."

I still hate hearing that title. I'm thankful for it, but despising it all the same.

With his two agents in tow, they leave us alone in the tent.

"That went better than I assumed it would. I thought for sure we'd have cuffs laid on us," Cap states, uncapping a bottle of water.

I have to say that now, personally knowing a little more about what he's done with his life, it's put a few more pieces of the puzzle together.

"If it's all right with you two," Trigger pipes in, grabbing our attention, "I'd like to get back to your clubhouse and grab Radish. She has to be wondering where I am."

I don't know much about dogs and their love for their humans, but I can't disagree that I have a girl waiting on me too. "Yeah. I'll drive if you wanna wait a sec."

"Yeah, I'll wait outside then." Turning to my brother, he holds out a hand. "Cody, I hope we can work things out between the clubs."

Taking the offered hand, they shake before he walks out, leaving us alone.

Sipping at his water, Cody caps the bottle. "We good, Agent Guierra?" he asks.

I scoff. "Yes, Staff Sergeant Guierra."

"Best we don't let on to the rest of the guys at the clubs that a DEA agent, military black op and Marine are in their midst. They may not understand." Cap is serious, dead serious we shouldn't tell others about his *credentials*. I have a different mind about it. If we want to make the clubs better, we need to give them the information to decide if the straight and narrow is how they wish to go. I won't lie further.

But.

I understand his trepidation. Not everyone will agree. Not everyone will understand that we're the government they've fought against.

"We'll talk about it later," I state calmly.

"Fine, we'll talk, but don't expect to have a club after. I think it will divide things pretty decisively. *You're* the head of your club and I mine. We'll work what's best for us each."

Uncapping the ninth bottle of water, I down it. The refreshing cool is perfect. My throat hurts from talking so much, and I'm grateful for the medic they had on hand, but I'm tired. I need to get out of here for a bit of rest. And sex. I want that woman wrapped around my cock.

Before leaving, I ask, "BBQ at my club tomorrow. Think you can make it?"

He smirks. "Yeah, I'll be there."

As I watch him walk out, I gather up my wallet and credentials and start for the door. Walking across the lot, staring at the carnage that's brought out to the coroner's vans, I'm glad that we survived. It sucks that Cody has gone through everything he has, and that our dad is gone, but we both know it's for the best.

Opening the door for the truck and hopping in, I find Trigger scrolling through his phone.

"Ready, man?" I ask, starting the truck.

He answers, not even taking his eyes from the screen. "Yeah."

Chapter

O **ubliette**

Jazzy, Death, and I left the warehouse before all the government stuff went down. Driving to Humble, the Army's repairman met us to fix up his leg. Bennett sucked back at least a bottle of Jack straight while they searched out the bullet. He passed out a few hours ago. Jazzy and I needed showers and a change of clothes, and more importantly, I need Lucius.

Washing up at Humble, I feel human again. The scars are internal now, but I still feel coated in filth.

"This is fucked. You know this is fucked, right?" Jazzy states as we're doing our make-up in the mirror.

"I'm grateful we're alive."

Blowing out a heavy breath as she's applying mascara, Jazzy pauses. "I've always expected I could lose Bennett or the boys, but not you. I was so scared of losing you. You're the closest thing I have to a sister, O. With everything, I don't think I would've done well with losing you at all." With a climactic pause, a lone tear drips down her cheek. "Fuck. Now I have to redo this."

I know her having to redo her make-up is just a diversion tactic. "Jaz, I was so scared I'd lose you too. I mean, once in that warehouse was enough for me, being in there a second time—" I choke on the words. "I didn't think we'd survive."

Smiling, she turns from the mirror and looks at me. "We did. We're strong bitches. We didn't have to kick ass, but we survived."

It's a statement, a testament to our will to live. It doesn't require a reply, so instead, I hug her tightly. "There's no one else I'd rather be kidnapped twice with than you, Oubliette."

"Ditto, Jasmine."

Hugging until the tension of the past few hours dissipates, we finish getting dressed and walk out to the club floor.

Walking in, I'm relieved when I see Miss and Trigger joking and getting on. Yeah, Trigger talking is a surprise, but one I'm glad for. He's always been so aloof and quiet. This craziness seems to have brought him out of his shell.

Walking over, I ask the only question I need to. "How'd it go?" I know Miss was going back to the clubhouse to clean up there, and that Trigger was staying with Cap and Lucius, so for him to be here, that means something.

"Good." He smiles. "I left Radish back at the clubhouse to come get you. She's found love in some monster, three-legged Mastiff named Kessel."

Monster is right. I'd almost forgotten about leaving my brother's dog at the club. With everything, the damn thing has either starved or been overfed. And if he's fallen for Radish, Grady will have a hard time getting Kessel back. I doubt he wants to fight Radish over her man to drag him home. I've seen that dog pissed off, and there's no way I would get in the way.

I turn to Jazzy for a goodbye hug. "See you in a bit?" I ask.

"Why? She's coming too. Busta's orders," Miss informs me with a wide grin. "Trigger and I will get Death. You two, go get in the truck."

Sweetly surprised, the two of us start for the doors. No one has to tell me twice that I was ordered by Busta. I need to see him. It's a driving force. I need to know he's okay and to see it for myself.

The ride over for the most part is uneventful. Bennett, in pain, consistently grabbed up the bottle of Jack. Swilling down mouthfuls along with painkillers, it tells me he's dealing with a world of hurt.

Seeing the clubhouse gates, with the invisible, yet mental stains on the ground, I feel myself tighten. There's no blood in the area where King knocked Sinew and the twins out, but my mind sees the destruction all the same. There's no way anyone can get me to go to the bathroom or walk down the hall to the residences. The memories of those deaths, of Panna and of Scarlet, are just too painful. I'll walk down the street to a house if I need to relieve myself, thank you.

Hopping out of the truck, the sound alerted the masses that we'd arrived. As Radish rushes out from around the buildings, Kessel hot on her heels, the two of them bombard Trigger with love. Jumping for kisses, circling him and rubbing against his legs, it's easy to see why he left her here. Once Kessel is content that he's given Trigger everything he should, the big dolt comes to me.

"Yeah, yeah. Hi, Kess, you big idiot." With all this bullshit, I appreciate life and how crazy it's been for me that much more.

Pushing away and running after Radish, Kessel bounds off in his three-legged gait. Which leaves me to search out Lucius. Steeling my heart, guarding my soul and pulling in all the strength I have, I pull the door to the clubhouse open. The defused light splashes the space. The once joyous area is in mourning. Everyone is somber and saddened. I don't blame them. There was no reason for Panna to die. Even now, I expect her light and airy persona to greet me as I enter.

Seeing a few familiar faces, the man I'm looking for isn't there. Retribution, slumped in the corner, slowly drinking himself into oblivion speaks up, "He's in church."

Which means to leave him the fuck alone. That's not somewhere I go. It's not my place. Starting toward the bar, as I move to take a seat, Quiver smiles weakly. "Why aren't you going to see him?"

"He's in church. I know the rules."

He laughs. "Sweet girl. *He's* in there. No one else. Go." He places two shots on the bar. "Take these with you. I have the feeling you could both use it."

Picking up the offered shot glasses full of liquid, I smile. "Thanks. When I get back, I'll return the favor."

Turning down the hall toward their sacred room—the place that business gets done—the door is wide open, and the large form of Lucius sits with his back to me.

"Lucius?" I ask with trepidation. Maybe Quiver was wrong. Lucius might like to be alone. After all, I know what happened. His world has been set to spin cycle—the axis flipped and he's in a heavy tailspin.

Turning in the chair, his body stiff, his stance is compacted and strained. Raising his hand, he calls me over. "Come here, Obi."

I start inside. "Shut the door, love," he states as a side comment. I bet his throat hurts like hell after the damage he took, and the interrogation he went through after. I left when he asked, but I saw the pain in his eyes that it ached to speak.

Laying the little cups from Quiver on the long table, I close the door and start toward Lucius after grabbing them back up. Stopping between his legs, offering him one of the glasses, he smiles softy as he takes it. Downing it quick and setting it on the table, I do the same.

Fire Whiskey. Quiver, the prick. He knows I hate that particular liquid. He'll get a Dirty Cocksucker for that later.

Bending low, concentrating on Lucius, I kneel on the floor before him, taking him in. He's not broken, he's upset.

"I never thought that it would come to that. I'd hoped that finding our family was going to be a good reunion, not one where you see your father killed all because he had no qualms about harming you. I always thought I was King's pawn. I was wrong. I was a pawn in my father's game. None of us really meant anything to him." Laying his head in his hands, he rests his arms on his knees.

Kissing his forehead, he accepts the sweet touch as he's warring with the outcome of today. Grasping his bearded face, softly stroking the skin of his cheek, Lucius leans into it. "You weren't a pawn. You were a player in his game, but you came out. You won. King, Rook, Queen—you took the board. The pawn can be a strong player if used right. You didn't lose it all. He did. You succeed and you'll live to make things better for you, your clubs, for everyone."

Pulling my hands from his face, Lucius kisses me as if I'm the last bit of goodness in the world. His tongue is soft and imploring, taking, but not rough. His hands hold me, but it's more like he's confirming I'm real. "Oubliette," he breathes out, full of need and desire. "I couldn't handle if you were hurt."

"I was fine, Lucius. Because of you. Because of what you did." He needs to hear it, to have a confirmation that his actions were the right ones.

Taking me again, Lucius' kiss morphs. From the sweet touch, to the feel I've come to enjoy. His determination to mark me as his is evident in the way his tongue wars with mine. Breathing into it, absorbing all the bad and accepting what he offers, I decide I want more. I want all of Lucius.

Breaking away, I kiss him gently on the nose, then on his lips once more. Moving my hands, unhooking the button on his jeans and releasing the zipper, I reach within. I have a need to remove all the bad thoughts racing through my head and replace them with good moments. Good thoughts. Good memories.

Grasping his warm heat, I wrap my hand as far around as I can, and slowly begin to move up and down. I'm teasing him, and I know he won't allow that for too long. He's a man of control. But I want control. I want to be the driver. I want to show him who's in charge—sometimes.

Pushing off his lap, resting on my knees, I pull his cock free from the confines of his jeans. "Sit back, Lucius."

He grins. "You don't have to tell me twice, woman."

Resting back as commanded, I pull his jeans lower so that the whole of his cock is uncovered. Bending above him with my mouth covering as far as I can, I move up and down with the strokes of my hand. He's more than my little mouth can handle, but I love the reaction that I'm pulling from him in this one simple little act. Looking up at him, seeing his head back and the wound on his neck visible, I know I'm not the only one who needs new memories.

Massaging the base, attempting to take more of him in, his hand comes around to hold my head in place. Stroke after stroke, he moves along with me, never pushing me too far, but guiding me. This is the first time I've done this with him, and I know he has to show me what's right for his enjoyment.

As he shifts on the chair, thrusting his hips out toward me, leaning into it, I know that what I'm doing is right.

"Christ, Obi. I'm gonna blow if you keep that up."

Isn't that the point, Lucius? I think to myself. But I continue my assault on him, hoping to give him the best experience possible.

With a harsh, "That's it," he picks me up off of him and stands me up, releasing the jeans I was wearing in a desperately quick motion. I'm standing in the room with only a thin tank top. Yeah, I changed at Humble, but my clothing options were still limited. This was the best I could come up with.

"Fuck me, Oubliette. You're beyond fucking gorgeous." Lifting my legs, he lays me down on the table, the tiny shot glasses zinging to the floor. With his mouth on my pussy and a hand on my breast, Lucius holds me hostage to his whims. It's amazing, and it goes straight to my core. Biting my lip to stop from screaming out—because we're in a clubhouse that's had enough death to think something's happened again—I feel every nerve firing in my body as his tongue swipes toward my release.

Just as I'm cresting, ready to explode, he rises up and slams his cock deep. "You're mine. No one else will touch this. I'll do everything in my power to keep you safe. Do you understand, Obi?"

Right now, I'd agree to being a sex slave in a harem if he asked. "Yes," I say, breathless and wanton between his thrusts.

"You are mine," he states with determination. "Be mine. Say it. Say you'll be mine. Wear my patch."

I hesitate. "Lucius..." As my climax takes me, I scream out, "Yes!"

While his end comes upon him, and his thrusts become harsher, then slower, Lucius lays his body across mine, fully sated and satisfied.

"You know, women aren't allowed in here. And sex on the table is strictly forbidden."

I giggle. "Good thing I have an in with the president."

Kissing me on the nose, he helps me to stand. "Yeah. Good thing."

Chapter

Busta

Walking back out after our mind-blowing sex, the common room is abuzz. The men stare at me wide-eyed, while the old ladies and whores smile. With Oubliette's hand in mine, I kiss her gently on the forehead and watch as she walks off to the bar.

Slipping behind it, she shoves Quiver in a playful way. "Had to give me Fire Whiskey. Don't worry, I'll get back at you when you least expect it."

Looking at the remnants of our club, the men we've lost, the kids that will climb the ranks, and everything we'll need to change, I figure there's no time like the present.

"Church, boys," I state authoritatively.

"Don't you want to give it a spray and wipe down first, Pres." Miss laughs, smiling and being his cocky old self. With an arm wrapped around a whore, he's settled back in after a day of death.

"Just grab the boys up, cocksucker. And the prospects too. Everyone in," I say, not taking the barb. Noticing that Trigger and Death are here, I ask, "You two in too?"

Yeah, I know. Another club in on church. It's more than odd. Today is a day for change, though. We might as well kick this off with a bang.

Slightly taken aback by the request, the two look at each other first. "Yeah. We're in, Busta."

Rising off the couches and chairs, boys trickle by me and start for the meet. With taps on the shoulder with either congratulations or a sorry, I nod and accept them all. Walking up with a limp, Death stops beside me. "You sure you want us in on this? There's still a ton of animosity toward the Army after True and Strike. Not to mention everything else."

"Brother's in blood is stronger than patches. Come on." I smack him on the shoulder as I help his limping ass to the room.

Ten minutes later, we're all settled, and even with the questioning glares, I know this will be a good thing.

Running down the events—starting with Obi, Panna, and Scarlet, then including the Cruel Intentions and Alta Noche, the boys of my club listen on, absorbing it all.

When I'm done, I open the floor for questions. "Anyone have questions or concerns?"

Silent brothers surround me, and it's unnerving.

Finally, Munch pipes up. "Busta, I've known you this whole time. If you were gonna let us rot in jail using the DEA, you'd have done it while DG was pres, or when True was pulling the bullshit he did with the Army." He looks to Death and Trigger. "I'm sorry for the parts we played in hurting your club. Family is sacred. True was wrong to do what he did, and I hope that Curse is doing better. I for one think you have it right, Busta. We need to work as a single club. A single ideal. I'm in."

"You know that means you might be voted out. You could be the low man on the totem—no offense," Miss states, looking at Death, joking about his heritage. It seems the two of them hit it off well.

With a smile and a returned quirky look, Death swills a few gulps of the bottle he's carrying around. "None taken, asshole."

"Then are you okay with that?" Miss asks us both. "I mean, it could be Busta and Death, or even someone else that could be voted as president of this ragtag bunch."

Looking at Death, knowing what we've talked about before the FBI showed up, I shrug. "I know. I'm good with it."

"Yeah," Death states with a smile. "For the good of the clubs, I'd do anything. Our families deserve us fighting for them the right way."

As the rest quietly talk among themselves, Retribution stands. He's not smiling, he's too broken for that. This has taken a heavy toll on him. "Busta, I'm sorry. I've lost too much to this. I need time to grieve."

Laying his cut on the table, I feel for him, knowing what he's lost. I can't deny him the request.

Moving toward him, picking up the discarded vest that is as much a part of Ret as his own skin, I hand it back to him. "You do what you need to, Ret. We're your family and we'll be here when you return."

As he walks out with rounds of apologies and condolences, he closes the door behind him.

Flight, being the smartass he is, pipes up cynically, "What would we be called? I'd hate to have to fix my tats and badges on the bike. I doubt you guys are up for it either."

As I'm about to answer, Quiver interrupts. "This will include the other clubs that were involved with your little shoot 'em up too, right?"

Scoffing at his question, Sinew, the pretty boy, laughs at Quiver. "Like you worry about real estate on your skin, Flight. Wondering about skin and stickers, that's a good one."

Flight and Quiver asking questions, tells me they're contemplating it. Sinew—not even patched in—wouldn't normally have a stake in this, but with us changing the landscape, prospect and patched is a blurred line.

"We hadn't really thought that out yet. Suggestions?" Death asks with a slight slur.

"The Brotherhood?" Fletch, the twin with the scar down his cheek, asks. It's the only way to tell them apart. As we turn collectively to look at him, he continues. "If you were to work as a collective on things that matter, and work as a team to gain profits—no infighting and no wars, then everyone wins. We've always put brotherhood above all else, why not be the Brotherhood and keep our titles? Be like the mafia. Each has their domains, but they work as a group. No cuts, no color, no changes."

Huh. Not bad.

As the boys talk amongst themselves, Death and I confer. "It's an easier way. Written as a coalition?"

Death nods his approval. "I'm good if you are. Then no one is the power. The combined strength is better. Think your brother will go for it?" he asks.

"Yeah. That I'm not sure of. We'll have to tread with Cap for a bit. Losing Raptor is a big blow. He'll need space." I turn to Miss, who's seated beside Trigger. "Think you can have a chat with Sinner? See if we can grab a meet in the weeks coming?"

"No idea why not. He knows we're all in this for the best of our businesses. It should be a no-brainer."

Asking one final time if anyone objects, we cast the vote.

Only three were decidedly against it, but the rest saw the positives of working as a group. Keeping our noses clean, losing the 1% and becoming stronger in legal dealings, this was a step forward for us, and not having to look over our shoulders.

With church ending and everyone spilling out, after talking so long, my throat was killing me. Thing was, it wasn't what was on my mind. The dull pain of it was minimized by the reminders of Obi's body laid out like a buffet on the church table. The only thing I have in mind is to get her home and fuck her until she can't even sit on my bike.

THE END

QUEEN

<u>Cap</u>

Returning to the clubhouse, finding the body of my best friend wrapped in a blanket and waiting for me at the door, I was broken in more ways than one.

I want to rain down hell on any in my way.

I want to bathe in the blood of those that caused this—but I can't. He's dead. He caused this pain and he knew what he was doing.

My father.

The man that I'd looked up to as a kid. The memory of the man that I modeled my life after. That when I'd left the Marines, I'd swore I'd find the camaraderie that I had when we were young in the Cruel Intentions.

That was what I needed in my life after all the death I'd seen on tour. That was what I'd always strived for, and Rap was at my side through it all.

I knew that the Marines had made me stronger, deadlier than any I knew, but Rap was my brother in arms, my brother in all that mattered. Blood didn't matter.

Now I'm adrift.

Falling to my knees before him, I can't feel anything. My nerves are shot, my soul is burning to the ground, and my heart is in shambles.

What I need is a woman. I need to pound this out. I need to destroy.

Walking into the club, seeing the despondent souls, those that understand what's happened and why I'm so broken. The rest, I explain it to them in church. I run down the family, the fight, the DEA and my involvement. When it's done, they walk out quietly to make the arrangements for Troy's burial. I can't. I'm too tossed to do it. There's no way I could sit in a funeral home and talk to them about what I need. I can't say goodbye to the only person who's been there for me. Everything would pale.

Seeing Maggie, my favorite girl sitting at the bar, I grasp her hand and pull her toward my room at the club. She doesn't argue. She understands exactly what I need. I need to mete out retribution on a body that can take it.

Stripping off her clothes quickly, attaching the cuffs on her ankles, neck, and her wrist, she waits for me to strap in her last free hand. Her hair is bound up, tied tightly for me to grasp if I need to, and her body is mine to command.

"Give me what you need, Code. I'm here." She sticks her ass out. "Use me."

Pulling a whip off the wall, I strike her hard across that globed ass. Her cries are swallowed up as she knows I don't like sound. Hitting her again, I see the truth of her need spilling down her leg. She loves this. She loves to be punished and abused.

Reaching around and pulling on her pert nipple tightly, her ass bows out toward my strained cock. I want to sink inside her, but not yet. I need more before I can. I need to forget everything.

Releasing her body, moving to my desk on the far side, I pull out the bottle. Picking up one of the pills, I slip it under my tongue. I want to forget everything. I need to be in a haze. Grabbing up a condom and walking back, striking her with the whip once more, I pull on the collar at her throat. It causes her body to bow so far that her ass is all I see. I place the condom on and thrust into her so hard, she almost squeaks.

"Maggie, I need your noise tonight. I need to hear you break. I want you screaming so loud they think you're dying. Do you hear me? Yell," I state softly, but with menace. Maggie nods her understanding. I thrust within her tight ass muscles without regard for her body. "I'm using you tonight to forget, to lose myself in you. Don't disappoint me."

Tilting the contraption that Maggie is strapped into, it pushes her to a horizontal position and allows me to hold her knees as holsters. I pump all of my madness and despair within as the drug takes hold. The darkness starts to creep in and my mind relaxes to the pain. Releasing one of her knees, wrapping a hand around her body and pulling on her nipples so tight, Maggie screams out, "That's too much, Code!"

But the sound doesn't register. Her cries are what I asked for. "Take it, Maggie. You want this and so do I. Take it."

"But it hurts," she cries out, so I release only to grab her collar.

"I said scream, Maggie! Fucking scream!"

Thrusting over and over, I let the dream of Troy alive and well watching on the bed fuel me. We used to share her. We'd take Maggie as brothers, giving her everything we had, and then giving her more.

I think of Troy. I think of all the times together. Of all the times we'd done just this. Lost in the memory, I reach my end on a haze of the drug.

I don't remember falling asleep.

I don't remember walking back to my house in the hills.

I don't remember anything.

• • • •

I DEFINITELY DON'T remember killing her.

Don't miss out!

Visit the website below and you can sign up to receive emails whenever Kerri Ann publishes a new book. There's no charge and no obligation.

https://books2read.com/r/B-A-SLJG-JSTT

BOOKS 2 READ

Connecting independent readers to independent writers.

Also by Kerri Ann

The Broken Bows
Rook
King
Pawn

Watch for more at https://www.authorkerriann.com.

About the Author

Mother of two insanely (well trained) sarcastic men, wife to a dangerously smolder inducing grumble bunny (fireman), and friend to some amazing ladies (you know who you are). Thanks for reading, thanks for being a friend, and I look forward to meeting you in the future for drinks, danger and laughs.

Living in Northern Ontario, Canada, Kerri loves to read, travel and find new reasons to write you fantastic love stories. Remember, not all love is clean. Dark, light, angsty, sexually charged and twisted—that's her genre.

It's heart wrenching stories where the muse directs her. As the instrument of their lives, their stories are told through piece by piece. You can hope for the good guy to win, but it won't always happen. She can't guarantee an HEA (happily ever after) or HFN (happy for now), because life doesn't always have those.

Enjoy the OMG's and tears. Tear your hair out, toss a book or two, because I want you to feel their pain too. As they live it, you can absorb it on the pages.

Website: https://www.authorkerriann.com

Goodreads: https://www.goodreads.com/author/show/15556808.Kerri_Ann

BookBub: www.bookbub.com/authors/kerri-ann

Instagram: www.instagram.com/authorkerriann

My Website: www.authorkerriann.com

Facebook page https://www.facebook.com/LoveandDreams

Twitter https://twitter.com/Daresanddreams

MeWe https://mewe.com/i/kerri/ann

Book+Main Bites https://www.bookandmainbites.com/kerriann

Tumblr https://www.tumblr.com/follow/authorkerriann

Read more at https://www.authorkerriann.com.